**One second, Kel...
the hayloft door...
next, her body slammed into a wall of
solid muscle.**

Hank snugged her against his broad chest. His strong arms wrapped around her waist.

Memories from the distant past crowded forward. They'd been teens then. Inexperienced. Awkward. Easily swayed by raging hormones.

But there was nothing awkward about the man who held her now. Nothing inexperienced, either.

His grip on her tightened until she tilted her head, and when his lips came crashing down on hers, it felt like the most natural thing in the world to open to him. For a long minute, she gave herself to the touch, the taste, the feel of him. "Hank, I..."

"Shh, baby. For a moment there, I thought I'd lost you."

But he had lost her. Long ago. And giving in to whatever was going on between them now couldn't happen.

Dear Reader,

The Circle P Ranch is home to a thousand head of cattle whose bloodlines trace back to the days of the conquistadores. It's a land where tall green grass stretches unbroken to the horizon. A place where brilliant pinks, purples and golds color the clouds at sunrise and sunset. I'm thrilled for the chance to take you back to the Circle P in *His Favorite Cowgirl,* my second book in the Glades County Cowboys series.

I'm glad, too, for the opportunity to share Hank and Kelly's story with you. For a dozen years, these high school sweethearts have done their best to forget the one they left behind. They've even convinced themselves that they've moved on, that they no longer want or need each other. But *His Favorite Cowgirl* is all about second chances. After a dozen years away, Kelly comes home, hoping to heal the rift with her grandfather. Meanwhile, Hank sees his daughter Noelle's visit to the Circle P as his final chance to prove he's a good dad. When circumstances force Hank and Kelly to work together, they give love a second chance.

I hope you enjoy reading *His Favorite Cowgirl* as much as I enjoyed writing Hank and Kelly's story. Many, many thanks to my cousin Paula Crews, whose love for her South Florida ranch inspired these stories about the Glades County Cowboys. Thanks, too, for the support of my Writers Camp pals—Roxanne St. Claire, Kristen Painter and Lara Santiago.

Leigh

HIS FAVORITE COWGIRL

LEIGH DUNCAN

HARLEQUIN® AMERICAN ROMANCE®

Recycling programs
for this product may
not exist in your area.

ISBN-13: 978-0-373-75540-0

HIS FAVORITE COWGIRL

Copyright © 2014 by Linda Duke Duncan

This edition published by arrangement with Harlequin Books S.A.

For questions and comments about the quality of this book, please contact us at CustomerService@Harlequin.com.

Printed in U.S.A.

www.Harlequin.com

ABOUT THE AUTHOR

Bestselling author Leigh Duncan writes the kind of books she loves to read—ones where home, family and community are key to the happy endings we all deserve. Married to the love of her life and mother of two wonderful young adults, Leigh lives on central Florida's east coast.

When she isn't busy working on her next story for the Harlequin American Romance line, Leigh loves nothing better than to curl up in her favorite chair with a cup of hot coffee and a great book. She'd love to hear from you and invites readers to follow @leighrduncan on Twitter, visit her Facebook page at LeighDuncanBooks or contact her through her website: www.leighduncan.com.

Books by Leigh Duncan

HARLEQUIN AMERICAN ROMANCE

For Reese Noelle

You make my heart sing.

Chapter One

Hank Judd urged Star forward until palmetto fronds no longer rustled against the big gelding's front legs. He spotted a grey Brahman in a patch of scrub brush and slapped a lariat against his thigh. "Get on, gal. Get on now."

Her calf at her side, the cow broke from her hiding place. As the newcomers trotted into the open, cow dogs worked them toward the other intruders Ty and Hank had culled from the herd of prized Andalusians.

"I think that's the last of 'em." Hank moved into place beside his friend and owner of the Circle P Ranch. Slowly they drove the Brahmans away from the main herd, while the dogs kept strays from wandering off.

"For now." Ty Parker removed his Stetson and mopped his head with a blue bandana. Fall or not, temperatures hovered above ninety degrees with the humidity so high a man could practically wring water from the air. "Till the next time Ol' Man Tompkins's cows decide the grass is greener on the Parker side of the fence."

Hank let his gaze sweep over the pasture on the far side of recently repaired barbed wire. The cattle had it right—the Circle P's grazing land *was* greener.

"Looks like Tompkins could stand to treat his grass

with fertilizer and weed kill, doesn't it? Those soda apples are takin' over his place." Wide patches of leafy green tropicals dotted the neighbor's acreage. The weeds sported wicked thorns no self-respecting cow would go near, much less eat. Looking for something more appetizing, Tompkins's cattle regularly pushed their way onto the Circle P land, where they helped themselves to the better-tended grass. And if the Brahmans happened to get impregnated by one of the Circle P's purebred bulls while they were visiting, so much the better.

Better for Ol' Man Tompkins, that was. The old rancher only gave lip-service to preserving his herd's bloodlines. Truth was, every mixed-breed calf put money in his pocket, no matter whose bull sired it. Especially since his Brahmans fetched a lower price at auction than Ty's sturdy Andalusians whose roots traced back to the first cattle brought to the New World by the conquistadors.

Hank clucked to Star as Ty moved ahead. The two men urged the half-dozen intruders along the trail toward Tompkins's front gate. The plan called for Hank to deliver the cows to one of the pens near the main house while Ty had a heart-to-heart with the neighbor, who had apparently decided not to do his fair share of fence mending.

"I'm glad you're here to take over for Colt." Ty's voice rose over the jangle of metal from the horses' bridles, the rustle of grass, the occasional warning growl from one of the dogs.

Hank swigged water from his canteen and stared at the distant horizon where the flat terrain met the sky. He shouldn't be here. He wouldn't have been…if he could've saved his real estate company in Tallahassee from going belly-up. He swallowed. The hows and whys of his presence on the Circle P were nobody's business but his own.

The cows stirred dust into the air. It clogged his throat, and he cleared it. Four generations of Parkers had raised cattle in this particular section of South Florida. Judds had worked alongside the owners for just as long. Hank and his brothers had vowed to carry on the family tradition after their father's death six months before. Each of Seth Judd's five sons had offered to shoulder the responsibility, but Hank's oldest brother, Garrett, had been sidelined by his wife's difficult pregnancy. As the next in line, Colt had taken a leave of absence from his job with the Professional Bull Riders to walk in their father's bootsteps. After he and the Circle P's new cook, Emma, had fallen in love, the newlyweds had purchased a spread in nearby Indiantown. For the past four months, Colt had spent his spare time overseeing the construction of his own house and outbuildings. His departure had opened the spot for a ranch manager, just when Hank had found himself in need of a job.

"You still think the twins'll move south sometime this winter?" Saddle leather creaked as Ty shifted toward him.

"Trying to get rid of me already?" Hank switched his reins from one hand to the other. His stay on the Circle P was only temporary. He'd move on just as soon as he got his feet under him again financially. The youngest Judds, twins Randy and Royce, called weekly to remind everyone they were chomping at the bit to take his place. Once they wrapped up their contract in Montana, they'd come home to co-manage the ranch.

"Nah. Just thinking about Noelle. It'll be hard

enough for her to settle in here on the Circle P. Harder still if she has to move again before the school year is out. You all set for her?"

Hank gulped. His ten-year-old was due the day after tomorrow. "Ready as I'll ever be, I guess. I sure appreciate your letting her join me here." His father's death had forced him to take stock of his life, and one of the things missing from it was a relationship with his only child. If he was ever going to make things right with her, he had to act. So, when his ex asked to send their daughter to boarding school for three months while she accompanied her parents on a round-the-world cruise, he had put his foot down for the first time since the divorce.

"Nope," he'd declared. "She's coming to the Circle P with me." And, thanks to a custody agreement giving Hank a say in his daughter's education, that had been that. Not that he could've afforded his share of the boarding school tuition, even if he'd wanted to.

One of the calves veered away from the rest of the cows. Ty waited till the dogs guided it back to its mama before he picked up the thread of the conversation.

"It'll be good to have kids running about the ranch for a while. Reminds me of when we were young'uns."

"Sometimes it seemed like there were more of us than there were cattle." Hank tugged his hat brim low enough to shade his eyes. As the middle of Seth and Doris Judd's five sons, he'd grown up on the ranch with Ty. Together with boys and girls from neighboring ranches, and a few townies, they'd played cowboys and Indians in the barn, feasted on watermelons and cantaloupes from the garden, caught fish and even tipped a few cattle when they thought they could get away with it…which they never had.

"Jimmy's gonna miss Bree when she moves." Ty ran his fingers through Ranger's mane. His son and the cook's daughter had become fast friends but, after six months of on-the-job training under Chef Emma, Ty's other children—foster sons Chris and Tim—were ready to assume responsibility for the kitchen on a day-to-day basis. Of course, Emma would still spend one day a week on the ranch, and she'd put in extra time during the winter and spring round-ups. But once she and Colt moved to their own place, Jimmy would lose his closest playmate. "Having another young person around here'll make it easier on all of us."

Hank frowned. "I don't know…. Noelle wasn't happy about boarding school. If anything, I think she's even less excited about coming here for the semester." Or spending time with a father whose involvement in her life had, until recently, been limited to occasional guest appearances.

"Ten's a hard age for kids. They're not little anymore. Not teenagers, either. It'll be good for her to get away from the city. Even if it's only for three months. She'll find out for herself what's important and what's not."

It sounded simple when Ty said it, but from the few visits he'd had with Noelle, Hank was pretty sure dealing with the preteen would be a challenge. He gathered his courage along with Star's reins. "If you don't mind my asking, how'd you do it with Jimmy? He was—what—five when he came to live with you?"

"Almost six." Ty shook his head. The boy had been abandoned on the doorstep of the Department of Children and Families where his wife, Sarah, had worked. "We've had our moments, believe me. Jimmy didn't think much of me at first. But then again, neither did

Sarah. The three of us, we kinda grew on each other."
With a knowing smile, Ty added, "It'll be the same for
you and Noelle. You'll see."

Hank expelled a harsh breath. He wished he had
Ty's confidence. He had busted his tail trying to provide Amy with the big house, the expensive cars, the
country-club memberships that she'd thought were her
due as the daughter of a millionaire. In the end, it hadn't
done a lick of good. Like the Tompkinses' cows, his
wife had moved on to greener pastures soon after Noelle was born. He'd convinced himself, or let his ex
convince him—even now he wasn't sure which—that
a good father sent his child to fancy summer camps,
enrolled her in expensive private schools, gave her all
the latest toys and gadgets. But the long hours Hank had
spent at work meant he was a stranger to his own child.
He stifled a laugh at the irony of his current situation.
He'd lost the business that had earned him the big house
and all the trappings of success, leaving him no choice
but to build a relationship with the girl he barely knew.

At the entrance to the Bar X, Ty dismounted. Hinges
in need of a good greasing squealed a sharp protest as he
pushed open the gate. Hank moved the cattle through,
and then held up while Ty swung the gate closed behind
him. Before he latched it, the two-way radio Ty wore at
his side squawked.

"Yeah," he said into the mouthpiece. A beat passed.
"He did what?" Ty's voice rose. He tugged Ranger to
one side as he reached for the chain securing the gate.
"I'll be right there," he said at last.

Hank left the dogs to mind the cows while he turned
to his friend. Beneath his Stetson, the man's face had
lost its color. "What's up?"

"I don't know how he managed to get up there, but Jimmy fell outta the hayloft. Sarah says he's okay— just had the wind knocked out of him—but she wants me to come home."

"Go. I got this." Hank swept his hat from his head and made a shooing motion. "I'll stop by the house when I get back. Let you know how it went with Ol' Man Tompkins."

Ty swung into his saddle. "Never a dull moment when there's kids around."

"I understand," Hank said, though he knew he probably didn't. He expected he would soon enough. He urged the cows down a weed-choked lane while Ty headed back the way they had come.

Thirty minutes later, Hank called out as he herded the Brahmans into the Tompkinses' front yard. He held his breath, hoping the crotchety old coot who owned the place wouldn't shoot him on sight. He had no desire to become the latest casualty of the long-standing feud between the two ranches. A move that wasn't completely out of the realm of possibility if the stories he'd heard at his daddy's knee were to be believed. For longer than anyone could remember, the Tompkins and Parker families had been at each other's throats. Legend had it the trouble began when the first owner of the Bar X had tried to dam the Kissimmee River. The move had all but shut off the Circle P's water supply, and the Judds had stood firmly beside their employers. Only once had there been a chance for a truce, but that hope had died more than twelve years before.

Cautiously, Hank swept the area for signs of life. Except for a cat slinking around the open door to the bunkhouse, nothing moved. Hank took a closer look, frowning at tools littering the ground beside a tractor. Paint peeled from the siding of the once pristine farmhouse. A broken front step, hay spilling from the loft— there were signs of neglect everywhere he looked. He dismounted and headed for the bunkhouse, hoping to find someone to take over the job of tending Tompkinses' cattle. But a line of empty cots stood before him when he stepped into a room that reeked of mold and mildew. He backed out, closing the door behind him.

With no ranch hands around, Hank crossed to a holding pen. He whistled, and the dogs herded the cows inside. He spotted the empty water trough, and was on his way to find a hose, when a horse trotted out from the darkened barn. The saddle on the silver gelding's back sent an uncomfortable shimmy through Hank's chest.

"Mr. Tompkins?" He raised his voice to a shout. "Anybody here?"

The horse wandered over and nudged his shoulder. Hank gathered the reins, which left faint trails in the dust.

"Hey there, buddy. Where'd you come from? Where's your rider?" He ran a hand down the horse's neck and across its withers. Relieved when he didn't find any sign of injury, Hank patted the long jaw. He frowned at the horse's rapid heartbeat, a sure sign of an animal in distress. "You thirsty?" he asked. Opening the gate to a pen where a mare had been turned out, he led the gelding inside. "I'll be back to get that saddle off you in a minute," he said. The horse snorted and trotted to the water trough.

At the entrance to the barn, the odor of stalls left too long without a good mucking stung Hank's nose. His breath grew shallow. As his eyes adjusted to the light, he spotted pitchforks and shovels in a haphazard stack. His lips thinned. Ty would have his hide if any of the men on the Circle P left equipment lying about, but it didn't look as if Tompkins cared.

Hank fanned the still air. Continuing to call out, he moved down the center aisle while he peered into each of the stalls. Dust motes danced in the air, but nothing else so much as twitched in answer to his shouts. He'd nearly given up on finding whoever had saddled the horse when a shaft of late afternoon sun broke through a hole in the roof. The light fell on a man's boot.

"Damn." Hank tugged his phone from his pocket, dialing before he took the first step. "We need an ambulance at the barn on the Bar X Ranch. Looks like Tompkins took a bad spill."

Slipping the phone into his pocket, he hustled into the stall. "Mr. Tompkins?"

No response. He tried again. "O—" He stopped himself. The neighbor had been "Ol' Man Tompkins" for as long as they'd known each other, but surely he'd heard the man's Christian name. He searched his memory, eventually coming up with the right one. "Paul. Paul Tompkins. Wake up, buddy."

Praying the old guy wasn't dead, Hank knelt down. Rheumy blue eyes stared blankly at the ceiling overhead, but the man's leathery cheeks were warm to the touch. He pressed his fingers against Tompkins's scrawny neck and found a pulse. A weak one, but there nonetheless. Looking for signs of obvious injuries, he studied the still figure lying on a thin layer of straw. The man's right leg bent at an unnatural angle, and Hank sucked in air. *Broken.*

"Don't try to move, Paul," he cautioned when the rancher moaned. "Help's on the way."

Spit dribbled from the side of Paul's mouth. His jaw worked. "Gaa-yee."

"What's that?" Hank leaned closer.

"Gaa-yee."

The slurred word sparked an image of a teenage girl with a coltish figure. "Kelly?" Hank asked.

The old man's blink told Hank he was on the right track. "Don't worry," he said, mustering his most reassuring tone. "You just lie still. I'll make sure someone gets in touch with her."

He would do it himself, but he'd long since deleted the number of the woman who had broken his heart. Twelve years later, he wondered if even her grandfather's fall would be enough to bring Kelly Tompkins home again.

FUELED BY A combination of truck-stop coffee and fear, Kelly Tompkins rounded the corner by the elevators. Nurses in turquoise scrubs and doctors in white coats filled the hall with entirely too much laughter for seven in the morning. Kelly waited until the group disappeared into the hospital cafeteria. Her empty stomach growled, but she headed in the opposite direction. There would be plenty of time to eat, comb her hair or wash up…after. Following the signs for patient rooms, she plunged through a set of swinging doors and stepped into the wing where the receptionist said she'd find her grandfather.

If he's lasted through the night.

The heels of her boots sent sharp echoes bouncing off the bare green walls. An aide in a uniform the color of cotton candy pushed an empty wheelchair past the nurses' station. At the far end of the hall, cafeteria workers grabbed breakfast trays from a tall cart. A strong antiseptic odor mingled with the scent of powdered eggs and burned coffee. Kelly pinched her nose, shutting out the acrid smells.

One hundred ten…one hundred fourteen…one hundred twenty. The door to room one twenty-two was closed, and she froze, suddenly uncertain if she dared go inside despite all it had taken to get there. What if, a dozen years after he'd thrown her out of his house, her grandfather still refused to see her? Or worse, what if she was too late? What if he'd taken his last breath while she was cutting across Louisiana? What if his heart had stopped beating when she'd pulled over for coffee outside of Gainesville?

Her hand shook so hard it rattled the door handle, but there was nowhere else to go, nothing else to do. She squared her shoulders, eased the door open and stepped into Paul Tompkins's hospital room.

Crisp white linens covered the empty bed. Folds at the corners of the mattress formed razor-sharp edges. Smooth, white, untouched, a pillow sat at the head of the bed. Movement on the nightstand beside it caught her eye. An ache swelled in her chest as she watched a drip of condensation roll down the side of a water pitcher. Kelly's breath stalled.

Was he…gone?

Tears filled her eyes. She blinked them away the same way she had brushed aside the sudden realization of how much she'd wanted this chance to finally make peace with the man who'd raised her. The man who'd kicked her off his ranch. The man who'd accused her of betraying the family name, and all because she'd had the bad fortune of falling in love with the boy next door.

Her grandfather hadn't spoken to her since. She wasn't sure if he knew or even cared that she'd broken things off with Hank Judd a month before graduation. That she'd parlayed an entry-level sales position into a desk in the corporate headquarters of Palmetto Boots, the largest family-owned boot company in America. She wondered if he'd think twice about the fact that she'd dropped everything, put her career at risk, to jump in the car and drive through the night to get to his side.

Had she missed her chance?

A sob lodged in her throat. She swallowed and tore her gaze away from the empty bed. Praying for some sign she was wrong, she scanned past a wide window and over the sleeping figure seated in a chair by the door. Her inspection stuttered and backtracked to a pair of worn boots. A shiver started at the nape of her neck and swept down her spine.

She skimmed slowly upward, over denim-clad legs to thighs that maintained their muscular shape even in repose. Her breathing slowed as she scrutinized a familiar chiseled jaw, the stubbled cheeks she'd once cupped in her fingers. The brim of a sweat-stained Stetson cast shadows across his eyes, and she expelled her breath, thankful she hadn't come face-to-face with one of her grandfather's sworn enemies—not to mention the man who'd betrayed her trust.

From the hall came the sound of muted voices. A cart rolled past the door, its wheels squeaking. The noise drifted into the room, where it disturbed Hank's slumber. His hat tipped back as he yawned, stretched and opened eyes that had always reminded her of clear blue water. For half a second, a lazy smile graced the lips she'd once loved to kiss. Then, awareness swam into his focus, and his lips straightened. The warm aqua eyes turned an icy blue.

"What are *you* doing here?" she whispered.

Ignoring her question, Hank uncrossed his ankles, leaned forward. His hands found his knees and he stood. "I see you finally made it."

The harsh tone hurt more than she'd thought it would, given the time and distance that had stretched between them. She hid her pain behind a cold glare. "Don't start with me, Hank. I've been driving all night."

Had the harsh brackets around his mouth softened ever so slightly? She peered up at him. Despite her own five feet, ten inches, he towered over her. There'd been a time when she thought his shoulders were wide enough to support the weight of the world. In truth, they hadn't been strong enough to bear the burden of the secret they'd shared.

"It didn't seem right leaving him alone all night, so I stayed." He mopped his face with one hand. "Must'a nodded off for a bit."

"You're the one who found him, then?" Her gaze drifted down. The wiry chest she'd once laid her head against had widened considerably. So much so that she struggled to remind herself he wasn't the only one who'd changed since the last time they'd seen each other.

"Yeah. He must'a took a spill off his horse." His voice softening, Hank swept his hat from his head and ran a hand through hair that no longer brushed the back of his collar the way it had when they were in high school. "No tellin' how long he'd been lying there, or how long he would have, if I hadn't come by when I did."

"Is he—" she glanced fearfully at the bed "—is he gone?"

"Afraid so." Hank's voice softened. "They came for him about an hour ago."

She was too late. Too late to heal the breach. Too late to say goodbye. The room spun, and she swayed while eighteen long hours behind the wheel caught up with her. An inky blackness blotted her vision.

She blinked hard.

Hank's arms wrapped around her, lending her his strength, his support. She laid her head against his broad chest, automatically seeking the firm plane over his heart.

"Hey," he whispered. "Steady now."

NOT QUITE CERTAIN how he'd gone from sparring with the woman who'd stomped his heart flat as a dried out cow patty to hanging on to her lest she collapse into a puddle on the floor, Hank sank his chin into Kelly's silky hair. He wrapped his arms around her, wondering at the narrowness of her frame, the slight indentation between her shoulder blades. She trembled, and he rubbed her back, murmured soothing words. He drank in the fragrance of lilac, which carried him back to the feel of straw and of Kelly beneath him as they made love in the Circle P's hayloft.

"The docs here know what they're doing. You'll see. They'll have his leg fixed in no time."

Kelly backed out of his embrace, taking her warmth with her. With nothing but cold air to fill them, his hands dropped to his sides while her eyes narrowed. He blinked. *Same old Kelly.* What had he said or done wrong this time?

Her lips thinned as she studied him. "You mean he's not… He's still alive?"

"Of course he is. It's just a broke leg." He winced, remembering the sharp angle of the break. He let his eyebrows knit. She thought her flinty grandfather was knocking at death's door?

Where'd she get that idea?

Hank swallowed a growl. He hadn't called her. Couldn't have, even if he'd wanted to. He'd long since rid himself of every reminder of the relationship that had burned so hot it'd consumed itself. The staff at the hospital hadn't notified her. It had taken some time to ride back to the Circle P, hop in his truck and hightail it into town, but he'd stopped at Registration before coming upstairs. That left Tompkins's personal physician, who, if he knew Kelly, would get an earful for making her drive through the night for something as simple as a broken leg.

"They'll set it," he said, mustering a reassuring smile. "He'll be laid up for a bit, I'm sure. But you'll see—he'll be back to his crotchety old self in no time."

"Yeah, that's what I'm afraid of." Kelly edged away from him until she reached the window. Blinking into the harsh sunlight of a new day, she folded her arms across her chest.

Hank waited her out. In truth, he was glad for the reprieve. He used the time to rub his palms together, trying to rid his fingers of the tingles that had arced through them when he'd taken Kelly in his arms. At some point in the dozen years since they'd last spoken, she'd lost the tan that came from spending days on end beneath the Florida sky. Tiny lines etched the corners of eyes that were more green than hazel. The sandy-blond hair remained the same, but it was longer. Even as he watched, she loosened the clip holding it in place. A waterfall of thick hair cascaded onto her shoulders. It spilled farther south until the ends swayed slightly above the waist of skinny jeans that were never intended for mucking stalls or herding cattle.

He scrubbed a hand along the side of the Wranglers he hadn't bothered changing in his rush to get to the hospital. "Time for me to get movin'." He'd had his fill of women who were all surface and glitter, from the tips of their rhinestone-studded boots to their curve-hugging shirts. Women like Kelly.

"Thanks for all you've done. I know Pops will— he'll appreciate it." Kelly continued to stare through the double-glass panes. "I'll swing by the Bar X on my way out. Leave orders for the hired hands to keep things running until he's discharged."

"You're not staying then?"

"At the Bar X?" She turned, a wistful look playing at the corners of her mouth. "Not hardly. He won't want me there, not unless the fall knocked some sense into that stubborn old mule."

She looked up at him, her glance searching for reassurance that wasn't his to give.

"Well, then." Hank toed the tiled floor with one booted foot. He paused, wavering between telling her what he knew and letting her figure things out for herself. "Look," he said at last, "I can ask around, but it didn't look like he had anyone working for him. The bunkhouse was deserted."

Kelly's eyes widened. "That's impossible. Pops always had a good-size crew."

Hank ran his fingers over the brim of his hat. It'd

take a dozen men to keep a spread the size of the Tompkinses' place in tip-top shape. Which, when he stopped to think about it, could account for all the signs of neglect he'd noted on the Bar X. He took a breath. How the neighbors ran their ranch wasn't any of his business.

"Tell your grandfather everybody's—" He bit his tongue. Paul Tompkins was better at making enemies than friends, so saying they'd all be praying for a quick recovery was pushing it a mite. He clamped his hat on his head. "I'll stop by the ranch on my way home. Make sure the cows and horses are tended to. It's the neighborly thing to do," he added over Kelly's protests.

He made it halfway to the door before it swung open. A doctor wearing green scrubs stepped into the room. His gaze swept past Hank.

"Ms. Tompkins?" The doc tugged a paper cap from his hair. "I'm Dr. Sheffield, your grandfather's surgeon."

Kelly grabbed Hank's forearm. "Stay, Hank. Please?"

It was a good thing he'd worn long sleeves, he told himself. Otherwise, her touch might have branded him. One glance and he knew he didn't have it in him to refuse her. Maybe later, when he'd gotten a good night's sleep and had had more to eat than a stale pack of crackers from the vending machine down the hall. But not now. Not when the grim look on the doctor's face made him think Kelly might appreciate some support.

From an old friend. A neighbor. And nothing more.

He shrugged. "Sure."

Dr. Sheffield propped one shoulder against the wall. "I inserted pins to immobilize your grandfather's leg until it heals. He's still in Recovery, but you should be able to see him in another hour or so. We'll remove the cast in six to eight weeks."

Fatigue etched its way deeper into Kelly's face. "Thank you, doctor," she whispered. "I'm sure he'll be glad about that. How long will he need to stay in the hospital, do you think?"

"We'll keep him here for another two days before discharging him to a rehab facility. The leg will need to be elevated and completely immobilized until the cast comes off."

Hank could practically see Kelly packing her bags and climbing behind the wheel of her car. As long as her grandfather was in rehab, the old man wouldn't need her help.

"After that…" The doctor peered at her. "Have you considered which nursing home you'll use? The best ones have waiting lists. You'll want to get him on one now."

"Nursing home? For a broken leg?" Kelly's eyes turned a darker shade of green. "I thought he'd go home. Maybe with a nurse or…" Her voice trailed off when the doctor shook his head.

"Hasn't anyone discussed his condition with you? Dr. Payne, the neurologist? Or Dr. Stewart, his general practitioner?"

"I live in Houston, Dr. Sheffield. I've been traveling all night to get here. I only arrived a few minutes ago."

"In that case… " Sheffield swept a quick look around the room. "Maybe you should sit down."

"Thanks. But I'll stand, if you don't mind."

Hank's hand found Kelly's shoulder. He squeezed gently, letting her know he was there for her.

"Ms. Tompkins, I'm afraid your grandfather has experienced a cerebral hemorrhage. In layman's terms, a stroke. His neurologist, Dr. Payne, ran a CT scan and an MRI, both of which confirmed the diagnosis. It appears there's been significant damage. We won't know the full extent for another twenty-four hours. Until the patient stabilizes. We do know he's paralyzed on the right side. We believe he's aphasic." At Kelly's frown, he clarified. "It's not unusual. Some stroke patients lose the ability to speak, or to understand anything said to them. What little your grandfather has managed to say is gibberish."

"You're sure, doc?" Hank asked, giving Kelly a moment to recover. "Paul, he spoke earlier." The old man had mumbled Kelly's name. At least, he'd thought so at the time. Hank ran a hand through his hair. At the doctor's skeptical glance, he reached forward. "I'm Hank Judd, Dr. Sheffield. I'm the one who found him."

"Too bad you didn't get him to us sooner. If you had, there would have been drugs we could have used to break up the clot, but—" Sheffield cupped his chin "—by the time he got to the hospital, the damage was permanent."

Hank fought the urge to double over. Maybe he should have slung the old guy on the back of his horse instead of waiting for the ambulance to arrive.

Ignoring him, the doctor turned to Kelly. "They'll work with him in the rehab facility, of course. With the right kind of therapy, your grandfather may regain some of his motor skills. But the prognosis isn't good. You should start thinking about where he'll get the long-term, full-time care he'll need."

Beneath his hand, Hank felt Kelly stiffen. He leaned toward the woman whose posture had hardened. "I'm sorry, Kelly," he whispered.

"You should leave now." She stepped away from him,

dropping her shoulder bag on the bed. "The doctor and I have a few things to discuss. My grandfather's condition is a private family matter."

A family he didn't belong to any more than she did his. Once upon a time, he'd thought they'd had a future together. But that was before he'd made a stupid mistake. She'd ended it then without giving him a second chance. Much like she was closing the door on his help now.

Guilt tore at him, but Hank refused to let it show. He straightened his Stetson and marched out of the room without asking the question foremost on his mind. Would she stay now, or would she go?

Chapter Two

Kelly held her breath while the hospital caseworker pursed brightly painted lips. After spending far too long consulting her clipboard, the woman finally added, "Your best bet is to get in touch with your grandfather's attorney. Find out if Mr. Tompkins has a care plan in place."

A half hour into a conversation in which she felt increasingly out of her depth, Kelly gave the woman a relieved smile. Margie Johnson had finally made a suggestion she could follow. "He always used Jim Buchanan over on the coast. I'll call him today."

"Good. That's good." Margie gave the empty hospital corridor a quick study. She leaned forward, her features softening. "I really shouldn't say this," she whispered. "I'm overstepping my bounds. But if he hasn't already named someone, don't leave it up to the courts to assign a professional guardian. Those people will bleed the estate dry, then stick your grandfather in the cheapest facility they can find. I could tell you horror stories." Margie drew back, sighing. "In times like these, we always prefer it if a family member steps in."

This just gets better and better.

"I'll look into it. Maybe he already has someone."

Though, considering her grandfather's surly attitude and the long-standing bitterness he'd held toward his closest neighbors, Kelly didn't think it likely. She combed her fingers through her hair, pushing it off her face. A trip to West Palm would delay her return to Houston, but did she have a choice?

Though he'd never bothered to hide his resentment, her grandfather *had* kept a roof over her head when no one else would. Looking back, she knew he'd had it rough—a widower trying to raise his granddaughter on his own. Would things have been different between them if—just once—he'd told her he loved her? If he'd said he was glad her mother had left her behind when she'd taken off for the last time? Or given any indication he knew, much less cared, how often his granddaughter cried herself to sleep at night?

He hadn't. Instead, he'd treated her like any other chore on his South Florida ranch, all the while criticizing her every move. He'd objected to her friends, her clothes, her attitude until she'd given up any hope of ever pleasing him.

Still, didn't she owe him?

Not that she had the time. No, she needed to get back to Houston, where final negotiations were underway for the big account she'd spent the past six months landing. She had to be there. Had to make sure every *t* was crossed, every *i* dotted. There was too much riding on this deal. Signing a major client would earn her acceptance into the Palmetto family. It would mean she'd finally have the financial security she'd worked for since the day she took that entry-level position stocking shelves. That she'd never again have to rely on someone who might let her down the way her grandfather had. The way Hank had.

Stepping into her grandfather's room, Kelly sank onto the chair beside the bed. The wrinkled neck and sunken cheeks above the stark white sheet had to belong to someone else. Not to the grandfather who'd ruled his household and his ranch with an iron fist. This man's hand lay lifeless at his side. His coarse gray hair fluttered with his every exhale. Kelly leaned forward and brushed a few wisps off his forehead.

"Did you miss me, old man?" she whispered.

She straightened his oxygen tube. She'd give him one thing: Paul Tompkins could hold a grudge. He'd never had a good word to say about the neighbors who, he claimed, had stolen the Bar X's water rights fifty years earlier. More recently, her grandfather had blamed the families next door for his wife's death in a car accident. Every insult or slight, whether real or imagined, had only deepened his hatred for the Judds and the Parkers. And he'd never forgiven her, either, not since the day he learned she'd crossed the line—fallen in love with a boy from one of the families he despised above all others. As punishment, her grandfather had kicked her out of his house the day she graduated from high school. The figure on the bed moaned. Kelly withdrew her fingers.

If wishes were horses...

The doctors said he might never recover enough to heal the breach between them. Still, the time had come to repay the favors—slim as they were—he'd shown her when she was alone in the world. She'd arrange for his long-term care. She'd find someone to tend his ranch. But she couldn't do those things sitting beside a man doctors said might never walk or talk again. A man who, in all likelihood, would drift through the next twenty-four hours in a dreamless sleep.

She blotted a bit of drool from his leathery cheek and whispered, "See you later, Pops." Trusting the nurses to get in touch with her if his condition changed, she headed out the door. On the drive, she made some of the calls the caseworker had suggested. One landed her an appointment the next day with Jim Buchanan.

An hour later, she pried open the mailbox outside the gate to the Bar X. Bills and circulars slid across the seat as her sturdy SUV bounced over a drive in desperate need of grading and rolling. At the end of the road, she stepped from the vehicle onto hard-packed dirt in front of the house she'd once called home. Burnweed and chamberbitter had taken over the narrow strip of lawn she'd mowed once a week, every week, for eight years. She climbed carefully over the broken steps leading to the front porch. Her grandfather never locked the house, but humidity had swollen the door tight. Putting her shoulder into it, she shoved it open.

Stale, overheated air clogged her throat as she stepped into the living room. Little had changed since the last time she'd crossed the threshold. Maybe the floral print on the overstuffed couch in front of the window had faded a bit. A thicker layer of dust coated the end tables. A few more cobwebs hung in the corners. But ranching magazines and farm reports littered the floor around her grandfather's recliner the way they always had. The same braided rug covered the worn hardwood.

She stopped only long enough to draw open the drapes and hit the switch on the overhead fan before she made her way into the dining room. There, she added the day's mail to a growing pile. She rifled through a stack of bills, dismayed by the collection of late and overdue notices that had been sitting untouched for so long they felt gritty.

"What have you been up to, old man?" she muttered. The meeting with her grandfather's attorney was starting to take on even greater significance.

A wave of nostalgia swept her when she headed down a short hall into a room where once bright paint had darkened to dull beige. Their corners curled and yellowed, posters of pop bands whose fame had long-since faded dotted the walls. She made quick work of stripping the sheets someone had draped over the furniture before she pulled a worn pair of jeans and a T-shirt from her bag. As much as she itched to give the house a thorough cleaning, it would have to wait for another day. On her grandfather's ranch, the livestock always took top priority.

Her hair pulled into a no-nonsense ponytail, she headed outside. She strode across the yard to the cattle pen, where troughs filled with food and water told her she owed Hank another round of thanks. An approaching pickup truck meant she'd have the opportunity sooner than she had expected. Despite all that had gone on between them, her heart did a little dance when the tall rancher stepped from behind the wheel.

"Hey." She crossed to him, her hand outstretched in a neighborly fashion. Keeping her tone decidedly neutral, she said, "Thanks for seeing to the livestock."

She felt the press of Hank's calloused hand in hers and waited an instant. When no chills raced up her arm, she relaxed, certain time and distance had healed her broken heart. He'd crushed her, turned his back on her when she'd needed him most, and she'd moved on. Her life, her future, was in Houston.

"Not a problem." He leaned into the truck and emerged bearing a casserole dish in one hand, a large paper bag in the other. His lips slid into their trademark half grin. "Our cook, Emma, sent food. Let me take it inside for you."

Kelly sent a troubled look over one shoulder. "If you think it's bad out here, you should see the house. I'll spare you that." She hustled the food into the kitchen. When she emerged five minutes later, Hank was nowhere to be seen, but his truck hadn't moved.

She followed the clang of metal against metal to the barn, where the bitter smell of ammonia stung her nose and brought tears to her eyes. Wiping them, she swept a quick glance down a crowded center aisle. She noted tools and equipment in haphazard piles, bales of hay that should have been stored upstairs in the loft. Scum floated in the closest watering trough. The three stalls on each side of the aisle needed serious attention.

Hank was already hard at work in one. Grabbing a pair of gloves and a shovel, she stepped into the stall across from him. Muscles that had grown used to working out at the gym sent up a protest when she bent to remove the old bedding, but the routine came back quickly as she raked and spread fresh straw. Across the aisle, Hank worked without speaking until they finished the first set of stalls.

As they moved on to the next pair, Kelly stripped her gloves from her hands while Hank drank from a thermos.

"How's Paul? Any change?"

She twisted the cap on a bottle of water she'd grabbed

from the fridge. "He's still the same. The hospital sent in a caseworker. Margie Johnson. Do you know her?" When Hank shook his head, she went on. "She suggested I talk to Pops's lawyer, get myself appointed his legal guardian."

Hank grabbed his shovel and disappeared into the stall. His voice floated over the partition. "You'll be sticking around, then?"

Kelly brushed the back of one hand across her face. Though anyone else might have thought her high school sweetheart sounded indifferent, she caught the quiet awareness in his voice. More for herself than for him, she shook her head. "Only till I find someone to run things here. I'm not staying," she said firmly.

A shovelful of manure landed in the bottom of the wheelbarrow. She shrugged. Hank's interest had died as quickly as it'd flared, which only confirmed how little he'd changed over the years. She returned to the business at hand. "You say there's no one in the bunkhouse?"

"From the looks of things, it's been empty for some time." He answered without a break in his rhythmic shoveling.

Kelly struggled to keep pace. "It looks like he's been trying to run this place on his own. Has anyone at the Circle P said anything?"

"I'll ask." Hank's damp T-shirt had molded to his muscular chest. He swapped his shovel for a rake.

"You don't know?" Her grandfather might not have trucked with the Parkers, but neighbors usually kept tabs on one another.

"Haven't been here that long myself." Across the aisle, Hank piled soiled straw into the wheelbarrow before hefting the handles and heading for the back door. "I'm only filling in till Randy and Royce come back."

"It's hard to think of the twins being all grown up. They were still in elementary school the last time I saw them." Her motions slowed. Though she'd fallen out of touch with her classmates, she occasionally checked the high school's Facebook page, where, several months before, someone had posted Seth Judd's obituary. "I was sorry to hear about your dad." For the eight years she'd lived on the Bar X, Seth and Doris had shown her more kindness than her own relatives had. "He was too young."

A strained "Yeah, it sucks" was the only answer she got, as Hank dumped the load on the refuse pile. He pushed his way back down the barn's wide aisle. "Mom's at Garrett's. He and his wife teach school in Atlanta. Or they did till Arlene got pregnant. But things aren't going well, and Mom's there for the duration."

Problems with the pregnancy? Kelly sipped air. Praying Hank wouldn't notice the way her fingers had spread protectively over her belly, she turned away from him. "And Colt?" she asked over one shoulder, brushing aside the pain the same way she had every day for the past twelve years.

Metal scraped against wood as Hank moved into another stall. "He fell in love with the Circle P's new cook and got married last month. That was some wedding."

"I'm sure it was." But thinking of weddings only brought up more old pain. She turned aside, working without saying anything more until the sweet smell of fresh bedding filled the air. She stepped into the aisle while Hank trundled the empty wheelbarrow the length of the barn. At some point, he'd removed his shirt. Sweat glistened on his toned and hardened muscles. She couldn't help it when her eyes slid down his sculpted abs to the pair of jeans he wore low across his hips.

Despite a stern reminder that Hank had proven himself a fair-weather lover, her mouth went dry. Reaching for her bottle, she gulped the last of the water. The days when she had thought Hank Judd hung the moon and all the stars in the sky—those days were over. The life she'd built to fill the void he'd left waited for her in Houston. And the sooner she got her grandfather situated, the sooner she could return to it.

"WANT TO BRING the horses in?" A few hours earlier, the barn hadn't been fit for man nor beast, but a proper mucking and fresh bedding had put things to right. Or at least, right enough that Paul's big gray gelding and pretty little mare didn't need to spend another night in the corral.

At Kelly's nod, Hank stepped aside, letting her take the lead. As she wiped sweat and dirt from her slim arms, he shook his head. Who would have guessed the cool sophisticate who'd shown up at the hospital would match him scoop for scoop as they worked in the barn? At some point, Kelly had swapped ostrich skin, rhinestones and designer jeans for serviceable boots and a pair of Wranglers that managed to hug her slender frame in all the right places. Little by little, the superior attitude that had reminded him more of his ex-wife than of the first girl to win his heart had slipped away, as well.

Not that she was the same person he remembered. Though he caught glimpses of the freckle-faced teen who had lost her virginity with him on a blanket beside Lake Okeechobee homecoming night, she'd grown into a woman with ample curves. She'd smoothed and polished her soft Southern drawl since the days when they'd been a whole lot more interested in sneaking off to their spot behind the bleachers than sitting through Ms. Cunningham's algebra class. He wondered if she'd remained single, but quashed the idea that she'd stayed true to him. After all, she was the one who'd chucked their relationship aside over one admittedly stupid mistake. Convinced she'd come to her senses and one day want him back, he'd concentrated on the rodeo while he waited her out. But she hadn't forgiven him. Not then. Not ever. Instead, she'd split the day after graduation. She hadn't been back since. He didn't know a thing about the woman she'd become.

"Where do you hang your hat these days?" While Kelly clipped lead ropes onto halters, he hefted the gelding's saddle from a fence rail.

"Houston. I'm a regional manager for Palmetto Boots." She took off for the barn, the horses trailing her.

Working for the world's best-known boot manufacturer explained the fancy footwear she'd sported at the hospital. "Been with them long?" he asked, dropping the saddle onto a sawhorse in the tack room.

"Ever since Pops kick—ever since I left." She settled the gelding into one stall, the fawn-colored mare into another. "I started out stocking shelves. Took night classes. Earned a degree in business. Hard work and a little bit of luck put me on the fast track to the corporate level. I'm in the middle of negotiating a big contract with Ivey's."

Hank caught a hint of pride in her voice and figured she deserved it for nailing a contract with the largest chain in the South. "Good for you," he called, grabbing curry combs and brushes from pegs near the door. He'd always known she was meant for bigger things, though there'd been a time when he'd thought they'd conquer the world together.

Kelly checked the gelding's coat for burrs. "So how about you? Last I heard, you were rodeoing."

Hank whistled. "Haven't done that in…" *Ten years and eight months.* He straightened the frown that sprang to his lips. "Rodeo's no life for a family man. I sort of—" he paused, searching for the right word "—fell into real estate. Mostly in North Florida. The Tallahassee area."

"Sales, huh?" Kelly grabbed one of the curry combs he'd balanced on the top rail. "Never figured you for a suit and tie."

"It took some getting used to." He caught her arched eyebrow over the horse's hindquarters. She knew him well. Too well.

"Business must be good if you can take this much time away from it." She began brushing.

"I've done okay." Although not lately. A nationwide recession had all but sunk the housing market. Not that he'd admit those failures to the woman he'd once dreamed of building a future with, especially not when hers had turned out so well. "Let's just say losing Dad made me re-examine some things. I realized family had to come first. Mine needed me here, so here I am." He bit his tongue. From the shape of things on the Bar X, it looked as though her grandfather could use some help, too.

Kelly's green eyes pinned him. "My future is in Texas," she said, leaving no room for misinterpretation. She took a breath. "If you're in real estate, though, you must know the market better than I do. What's a place like this going for these days?"

"You don't want to hang on to it?" The Bar X had been in the Tompkins family far longer than the Circle P had belonged to the Parkers. He watched carefully as Kelly's gaze swept through the barn.

"I might not have that option. I found a couple of final notices from the tax office on the dining room table."

A trip to the hardware store and some elbow grease would fix broken steps and door hinges, but a man who didn't pay his tax bill could lose his birthright to the highest bidder at the county auction. He and Colt were going to the next one in…

Hank gulped. "You don't have much time. The tax sale is in three weeks. October first."

Kelly's hands, which had been working a comb through the gelding's long mane, stilled.

"Crap," she whispered at last. "How'd he let things get this bad? I was hoping to sell the ranch to pay for Pops's care, but…" A pair of expressive brows rose over rapidly widening eyes. "Those nursing homes the social worker mentioned—I spoke with a couple of them on my way out here. They're mighty proud of what amounts to three squares and a room. I've stayed in five-star hotels that didn't charge as much."

"That's down the road though, right? First, he'll be in rehab till his leg heals?" Hank worked a pick through the little mare's hooves. "The way I see it, your first priority has to be the taxes. You have the money?"

Kelly sighed. "I have enough in savings to pay the bill. It won't leave much."

He propped his elbows on the mare's back. "You pay those taxes. It'll buy you some time to figure out what to do next. Meanwhile, your grandfather's Brahmans have already overgrazed that pasture. They need to be moved." In a gesture that stirred a long-forgotten urge to be her hero, Kelly tucked her bottom lip beneath her teeth. He swallowed. "Look, the job's too big for one person, which is probably why Paul didn't get around to it. I can spare a couple of the boys for the day or so it'll take to move those cows. Any longer than that, though, and you'll have to clear it with Ty."

Tugging on the end of her ponytail, Kelly stepped back. She folded her arms across her chest. "I don't expect you to solve my problems for me, Hank. Ty, either."

"Hey, we're just talking." Uncertain where the conversation had veered off track, he held up his hands in mock surrender. "There was a time when we could talk about anything."

"That was different." Kelly's arms remained in place, her posture stiff. "We were friends."

He cocked an eyebrow. "We were a lot more than friends."

The gelding pawed the wooden floorboards as Kelly stared at a spot somewhere over his left shoulder. "Those days are done," she whispered. "I'm not interested in starting over."

"Me, either." Even if he was dumb enough to take up with a woman who'd walked away from him without so much as a second glance, with all he had going on this year, starting up with his old girlfriend again had *bad idea* written all over it.

"Just so you know," Kelly said, thawing a bit.

"No problem. I'm just trying to be neighborly." He

grabbed a brush and gave the little mare another rub down. While he worked, he explained, "Besides, you know the Parkers. They'll insist on helping with your grandfather's cattle till he's on his feet again." For good measure, he added, "Any of us would."

Kelly appeared to mull things over. With a sigh, she dropped her arms to her sides, the fight seeping out of her. "Sorry. I didn't mean to snap at you."

"It's all right." Hank scuffed one boot through the straw. "You've got a lot on your plate." He fought an urge to wrap an arm around her shoulders when moisture dampened her eyes. Neighborly kindness would only explain so much. Instead, he gathered an armload of curry combs and brushes. Stopping at the door to the gelding's stall, he glanced back at her. "So, we're good, neighbor?"

"Yeah," she said, running a calming hand over the gray's long neck. "We're good."

By the time the horses were fed and watered and the tools stowed properly, the sun had dipped beneath the horizon. In the distance, the last glimmers of daylight painted the low-lying clouds gold. Night birds winged across the sky, their calls rising above the drone of cicadas. From somewhere far off came the throaty growl of a bull alligator.

Hank paused for a moment, drinking in the view he'd missed during the years he'd spent in North Florida, where sunsets hid behind hills and tall trees. It seemed ironic that Kelly wanted to leave all this behind just as he was rediscovering it, but—he shrugged his shoulders—the choice was hers. He wasn't a part of her life anymore. Still, if she was serious about selling the ranch, he wouldn't mind handling it for her. Or earning the big commission the sale would generate. He leaned against his truck. Though the housing market had dried up, he still had contacts in Tallahassee who might be interested in the ranch as an investment.

"I'm more familiar with land prices in North Florida, but I'd be glad to run some comps—comparison sales—for you. It'll give you a good idea of the market." He gestured to the barn door, which, thanks to a broken hinge, tilted at an odd angle. "I can tell you one thing, though. You won't get top dollar without fixing the place up a bit."

"I have a meeting with Pops's attorney in West Palm tomorrow morning. I'll know more about what I can or can't do with the ranch after that."

"Oh, yeah? I'm going there myself. I'm driving over to pick up my daughter." Hank lifted his Stetson and ran a hand through his hair while he worked out the logistics. The two-hour drive into the city would give them time to hammer out a plan for selling the Bar X. "Maybe we can ride together and talk over those comps on the way."

Kelly's head rose. "You have a daughter?"

"Noelle. She's ten, going on eighteen."

Something dark worried Kelly's eyes. "You didn't mention you were married."

"Divorced," he corrected. "I met Amy while I was riding in the rodeo. The marriage didn't last past Noelle's first birthday."

"Didn't take you long to move on, did it?"

He winced at the accusation, but he couldn't argue. She was right. He'd practically bounced from the breakup with Kelly straight into Amy's arms. With her golden hair and a willowy figure so much like his first love's, the fan who'd walked up to him in a bar the night before the Silver Spurs rodeo had seemed irresistible. As it turned out, the two women were nothing alike, though Amy had kept her true colors under wraps for a while. It wasn't until after the wedding that he'd discovered his bride's family owned half of Tallahassee. A short while later, he'd realized she'd skipped over the faithfulness part of her oath to love, honor and obey.

He cleared his throat. "It was one of those whirlwind courtships you hear about all the time, but nobody thinks will happen to them. This one didn't have a happy ending." But that was a story for another day.

For a minute, he thought Kelly might insist on hearing the sordid details. He held his breath until, at last, she shrugged.

"Well, I best get moving if I'm going to have a handle on Pops's accounts when I meet with the lawyer."

"And I'll check out the local real estate tonight so we can go over some numbers on the way. Pick you up at nine?" Noelle's flight was due a little after noon.

"That works." On her way to the house, Kelly turned back. "Thank Emma for the casserole," she said. "And you for all your help."

Hank resettled his hat. Forgiveness wasn't a particularly strong trait in the Tompkins clan. He supposed, based on the harsh relations between their families, an uneasy truce with Kelly was the best he could hope for. But, watching her walk away, he couldn't help wishing fate had spooned just a smidge more forgiveness into the tall blonde's nature. If it had, he was pretty sure they'd still be together.

Chapter Three

One shoulder propped against the concrete wall in the arrivals area, Hank pulled a scrap of paper from his back pocket and consulted his notes. Noelle's flight had left Tallahassee on schedule that morning. According to the airline, she'd had plenty of time to make her connection in Atlanta. A glance at the flight status board told him his daughter's plane had touched down in West Palm half an hour earlier. But no flight attendant escorting a preteen had streamed past his vantage point. In fact, five minutes had passed since the last person had walked down the Jetway.

Had his daughter missed her flight? Worse, had she missed the connection in Atlanta? His heart clenched at the thought of his child wandering unaccompanied through the huge international hub. He pushed upright, his pulse thudding, as he looked around for someone in charge.

He spared a last glance down the walkway and spotted a thin slip of a girl flanked by airline employees. A welcoming smile sprang to his lips and he waved, but he might as well have saved himself the effort. Noelle's head remained down, her sandy-blond hair draping her face while her fingers flew across her cell phone. Hank heaved a sigh. So much for their happy reunion.

When Noelle lagged behind, the attendants exchanged exasperated looks over her head. Their heels sounded a harsh clatter against the marble as they prodded her along. Stopping at the entrance to the empty waiting area, one of them consulted a clipboard. "Mr. Judd? Mr. Henry Judd?"

An air of quiet desperation clung to the woman in the navy blue uniform. Hoping to put her at ease, Hank stepped forward with a slow smile. "Hank Judd. That's me."

Deliberately, Noelle reached for an earbud that dangled from a loose wire. She jammed the piece in her ear. Her voice louder than necessary, she announced, "Yes, I'm here. The plane landed *hours* ago, but the stewardess let everyone else off first. Really, Mom, you ought to complain. That was so not first class."

"Noelle!" Hank's back stiffened at his daughter's rudeness.

His ten-year-old looked up from her cell phone long enough to roll her eyes. "Whatever," she mouthed.

The flight attendant's rigid expression tightened. "I'll need to see your driver's license, sir."

Hank aimed a sympathetic smile toward the woman while he reached for his wallet. If a child he'd been assigned to watch had behaved so badly, he might have been tempted to hand the brat over to the first person willing to take her, ID or no ID. He checked his watch, not at all surprised to see that less than five minutes had passed, and he'd already gone round one with his daughter.

Without saying a word, the attendant jotted down

a few numbers and handed him the clipboard. Hank signed his name. The two women walked off, their suitcases rolling behind them. And, just like that, Noelle was his responsibility. He glanced at the child who continued to type.

"Noelle," he interrupted. "Thank the ladies."

Her mumbled response sounded a whole lot more like "For what?" than "Thanks." The minute they were alone, Noelle's lips pursed. "Internet service on the airplane was so bad I couldn't even text my friends."

"That's probably because you're not supposed to use your phone on the flight."

"Whatever."

As his daughter repeated a word he was already certain he'd hate by the end of her first week in South Florida, Hank drew in a deep breath. This was not the start he'd envisioned when he insisted Noelle come stay with him, but really, her reaction was exactly what he deserved. Determined to get things off on the right foot with his only child, he reached for the backpack slung across her shoulder. "Here, I'll carry this. Let's go get your bags. Where are your claim tickets?"

Noelle's feet remained rooted to the floor. "That's all I brought."

He hefted the bag, judging its weight. "Mighty light for a whole semester, don't you think?"

"I can send for the rest…if I stay." Noelle rolled one shoulder in a dismissive move she'd obviously copied from her mother.

Hank swallowed a quick retort. Noelle might be rude but she had a point. Until recently, he *hadn't* made his daughter a priority in his life. He'd been too busy building his business, chasing after the almighty dollar, to give his child the attention she deserved. Deep down, he'd known it was wrong to let Amy ignore their custody agreement. To give in when his ex-wife insisted Noelle would rather ski in Aspen or Vale than rattle around in his Tallahassee condo over Christmas vacation. Or that attending summer camp with her friends was better than hanging out by his pool.

All that had changed when his dad died. Both Amy and Noelle had skipped the funeral. Not long after, it had hit home that if he didn't want to spend the rest of his life a stranger to his only child, he'd have to make some adjustments. Noelle's coming to stay with him at the Circle P was the first step.

But what had he gotten himself into?

He gave his daughter a long, appraising look on the way out to the parking lot. By his estimation, the wedge heels she tottered along on were far more suitable for a teenage ingenue than for a child who hadn't celebrated her eleventh birthday. Her lace-trimmed leggings, which ended at mid-calf, wouldn't last through a day's work on the ranch. He tsked at the bra straps boldly displayed on each shoulder. A bra? Her body hadn't even begun to fill out. Was his little girl in such a hurry to grow up?

He shook his head. No matter what the answer, the situation called for a shopping trip.

"We'll stop in Okeechobee on our way back," he announced, sliding in behind the wheel. "Afterward, we'll grab a bite before we head to the Circle P." Cowboys had the best burgers in town and it was on the way. He put the truck in gear. "First, though, we have to pick up my friend Kelly."

"Kelly? You brought your girlfriend along?" Scorn

dripped from Noelle's voice. She flopped back onto the seat. "This whole trip sucks," she declared.

KELLY STARED THROUGH the tall glass windows over-looking the sidewalk. Briefcases swinging, attorneys in three-thousand-dollar suits blotted sweat from their foreheads as they hustled to and from the courthouse at the end of the block. She smoothed the tailored skirt of the one black suit she'd thought to throw in her suit-case and told herself she should join them. Should step from the air conditioned building where Jim Buchanan had his offices. Yet she couldn't make her feet move. Couldn't pry her fingers loose from their tight grip on her satchel long enough to push open the lobby door. Admitting the talk with her grandfather's lawyer had muddled her thoughts, she took a much-needed mo-ment to digest an overload of disturbing information.

Not for the first time since receiving the call that had upended her life, she wished she had someone to turn to. A friend. A confidante. Her gaze slid across the street to the truck parked beneath a tall palm tree. In the front seat, Hank leaned past the headrest to speak with his daughter.

In her teens, he'd been her go-to person. She'd been able to tell the tall rancher everything, share all her se-crets with him. Of course, that was *before* she'd had to face the consequences of giving in to a potent mix of first love and raging hormones. Before Hank had stormed out instead of living up to his promise to stand beside her no matter what. Yet, she missed their cama-raderie. Despite a decade of trying, she'd never shared that same connection with anyone else.

Could they get that easygoing give-and-take back

again? If only for a little while? It wasn't as if either of them planned to stay in Glades County. Soon, Hank would return to his business in Tallahassee. The minute she settled her grandfather's affairs, she'd head back to Houston. She wanted to believe Hank when he swore neighborly kindness, and nothing more, was behind his offer to help with the chores on the Bar X. After all, good neighbors shared their troubles. They even offered one another advice, didn't they? Surely, she and Hank had grown old enough, wise enough, *smart* enough to avoid anything deeper than friendship for the short time they'd be around each other.

A traffic officer pedaled slowly down the street. When he stopped to write a ticket for the vehicle behind Hank's, Kelly managed to get her feet in motion. Charging into the thick blanket of heat and humidity that passed for weather in West Palm Beach, she raised a hand.

"Hank!" At the first break in the traffic, she crossed to his truck. "Sorry. I hope you weren't waiting too long," she offered as the policeman rode past.

"We've only been here a few minutes." Hank's smooth tone calmed her nerves while she settled her satchel on the floor at her feet and slipped her purse from her shoulder. "Things at the airport took longer than I'd planned."

From the backseat came an accusatory, "I told you the flight attendant wouldn't let me leave. She treated me like a baby. I am ten, you know."

While Kelly buckled her belt, Hank exhaled slowly. "She was just doing her job," he said, his voice tightening. "If you'd gotten lost, she would have been in big trouble."

Kelly slanted a cautious look toward Hank before, with a renewed determination to act *neighborly,* she summoned a smile.

"Hi! I'm Kelly." Thin gold bands jangled lightly as she extended a hand. "You must be Noelle. Your dad has been looking forward to your visit."

With a brief nod, Hank spoke loud enough to be heard over his truck's throaty engine. "Kelly's grandfather is very ill. She came home to take care of things while he's in the hospital."

"Is he going to die?"

Though the bald-faced question nearly made her flinch, Kelly stopped to think. *Was he dying?* The medical staff stressed the need for long-term care, but they didn't know her grandfather the way she did. From sun up to sun down, the man had spent his life outdoors. Unless he could regain the ability to walk, to speak, she feared he'd lose the will to live. Her stomach clenched and she cleared her throat. "I hope not, Noelle."

"My grandfather had a heart attack last Christmas," the girl said. "He and my grandmother are on a cruise around the world while he gets better. My mom went with them. I was supposed to go away to school." She gave a sigh worthy of an actress on Broadway. "*Dad* made me come here."

Kelly winced as sympathy for the child squeezed her heart. Abandoned by her mom, convinced her father didn't want her—the kid's emotions had to be all over the map.

Noelle crossed her thin arms. "But don't get used to my face. I won't be here long."

The unease of years spent bouncing around while her mother moved from one low-end job to another, one relationship to another, rippled through Kelly's chest. She quirked a brow. "I thought you were starting school next week."

The child jerked her head toward her dad. "He'll send me back. He always does."

He always does? Kelly scoured Hank's face where guilt darkened his blue eyes. "Really?"

"Not this time."

His firm response did little to douse a sudden flare-up of old doubts, painful memories. Her mind flashed to the absolute relief that had flooded her boyfriend's face the night she'd told him she'd lost the baby. His baby. Noelle's reaction struck another blow against any hope that Hank's attitude toward family and children had changed over the years. Kelly sucked in much-needed air. She couldn't trust a man who didn't put his child above his own needs and wants. As for his daughter, she'd handled more than one entitled teen in her years at Palmetto Boots. The company gave so many of them entry-level positions that classes in dealing with diffi-cult employees were mandatory. Kelly turned even far-ther in her seat and studied Noelle until the girl made eye contact.

"Let's try that again, shall we? Only this time, I'd appreciate a bit more respect." She extended her hand across the space between them. "Hi. I'm Kelly."

Noelle's smirk fell from her lips. Her face reddened. "I'm Noelle," she said, blinking.

They shook while Hank put the truck in gear and pulled neatly into the flow of downtown traffic. "How'd things go with the lawyer?" he asked, as though the conversation between Kelly and his daughter had taken place in another vehicle…on a different planet.

Kelly glanced at the child, who had retreated to the farthest corner of the vehicle. A casual observer might think the passing scenery had captured the girl's attention. But blue eyes so much like her dad's glanced into the front seat often enough to prove that Noelle listened in on every word. Kelly shifted in her seat. Striking a businesslike tone, she said, "For now, let's just say it didn't go the way I expected. Not even close."

By the time they left West Palm's city limits, the faint strains of an unexpected country rhythm seeped from Noelle's earbuds. Kelly checked to make sure the child was bent over her cell phone before she pitched a low question to Hank.

"Did you have a chance to run those comps?" They had planned on talking about real estate that morning. Instead, she'd watched the flat land roll past, intrigued by how little the area had changed in the twelve years she'd been away. Oh, the State had resurfaced the two-lane roads. Hank's truck flew past a new gas station or two. Mostly, though, the long stretch between Okeechobee and West Palm remained home to dairy farmers and ranchers. Green grass stretched for miles, interrupted only by barbed wire fences and wide drainage ditches.

Hank pulled a folder from the center console. "Not too many ranches the size of your grandfather's have changed hands around here lately," he said, as she reached for it. "Developers have bought up the land around the cities, but so far, no one seems to be interested in building luxury high-rises in our little corner of the world."

"Thank goodness." She might not want the ranch for herself, but she couldn't bear to think of it being turned into a housing complex. She flipped open the folder. Skimming over land sales throughout South Florida, she felt her pulse quicken at the amount a neighbor had gotten for flood-prone acreage. "The Barlowe place went for that much? I had no idea."

"With your prime grazing land and good water, the Bar X should bring a tidy sum. Of course, the economy has taken a hit lately, and you have repairs to make. The house…" Hank lifted a hand. "I wouldn't put a lot of money into it. Most buyers will want to tear it down and start fresh."

"Pops wanted everything to stay the way Gramma left it." Come to think of it, Kelly had, too. She pictured worn fixtures and a decor that hadn't been updated in over twenty years.

Flipping to a page where Hank had estimated a price per acre, she swallowed. "Okay, you've impressed me." Her old boyfriend might not have been much of a father, but he knew his stuff when it came to real estate. "I guess this explains why the tax bill was so high." Writing that check had all but depleted her savings account. She glanced up. "I don't suppose there's any chance Ty would be interested in buying the Bar X."

Hank shook his head. "I asked him about it last night. He's stretched a little thin right now. Maybe in another year or two."

Kelly toyed with her bracelets. She couldn't wait that long. She needed a buyer, and soon. Her bosses in Houston had already called twice for updates on the Ivey's account. They'd made it clear she had to close the deal in order to secure her future at Palmetto Boots. Meanwhile, her grandfather's insurance would cover his care at the rehab center, but once he moved to a nursing home, the bills would mount quickly. The only way to provide him with the best possible care was to sell the ranch for top dollar. Preferably yesterday. With shaking fingers she smoothed a few strands of hair that had escaped from her sleek updo. She stashed the folder in her satchel. Though she intended to ask for more details on projected sales figures, Hank had slowed for the usual traffic buildup on the outskirts of Okeechobee.

"Next stop Eli's," he announced a few minutes later. He steered into a parking space and cut the motor. "Noelle packed a little light for her trip."

In the backseat, his daughter removed her earbuds. Her mouth gaped open as she stared at the fake hitching post that adorned the wood-frame building. "This isn't the mall," she protested.

"Judds have been shopping at Eli's since the day the store opened," Hank countered. "Trust me. They'll have everything you need."

He slipped the keys into his pocket as if that was the end of the discussion, but, from the way his daughter's face darkened, Kelly sensed a brewing storm. Hoping to ward it off, she aimed a supportive smile at the kid dressed from head to toe in designer labels. "It may not be couture, but I'm sure we can find something you'll like. Me, too. I was in such a hurry to get here, I only packed a few things."

Noelle's gaze bounced between the two adults. Kelly waited until, at last, the child pinned her with an appraising look. "Honest? You shop here?" she asked.

"Every chance I get," Kelly swore. Truth be told, when she'd been Noelle's age, she would have given her eyeteeth for a pair of jeans from Eli's. Her grandfather, however, had insisted that Goodwill was *good enough*.

Which, she guessed, explained the mail-order account she'd established after receiving her first paycheck.

"C'mon," she urged the child. "You can help me find some work jeans while we pick up whatever you need."

Indecision played across the girl's elfin face for a long moment before Noelle reluctantly set aside her electronic gadgets. "I guess I need some jeans to wear horseback riding."

Holding the door for his daughter, Hank mouthed a silent *thank you* over the roof of the truck. Kelly shrugged the comment aside. Beneath Noelle's false bravado was a kid who just wanted what every kid did—to be loved. A task her father had evidently neglected.

At the store's threshold, Kelly paused for a moment to drink in a welcoming blend of leather and linseed oil. She swallowed a smile when Noelle stopped in the middle of the aisle, apparently transfixed by the life-size posters of rodeo stars mounted on the walls. Eli's claimed to carry everything a modern rancher needed. With racks of clothes, boots and leather goods crowding the floor, the owners lived up to their promise. Left alone, Kelly knew she could spend hours sorting through the rows of sequin-studded jeans or shirts with Western piping along the collars. She stole a quick glance at the Palmetto Boot display and gave a nod of approval at its prominent location, while Hank strode to the counter without so much as a glance at the fringed buckskin jackets that made her mouth water.

"Hey, Mark." Hank nodded to the stocky clerk at the register. "You remember Kelly Tompkins, don't you?"

"Why, sure. We used to hang out at the Circle P."

Mark extended one hand for the obligatory shake. "Sorry to hear about your grandfather. He doing okay?"

Not at all surprised word had already spread thirty miles to the neighboring town, Kelly nodded. "He has a long, hard road ahead of him, but he's a fighter."

"Well, tell him we're all hoping for a speedy recovery," Mark said. "Now, how can I help ya'll today?"

"This is my daughter, Noelle." Hank's hand on her shoulder propelled the child forward. "She needs two—make that three—pairs of Wranglers, a couple of T-shirts, a pair of boots and a hat."

Mark nodded. "I think we can fix you right up." He cast a glance over Noelle, considering. "You're a mite on the small side. You wear a 7/8?" Without waiting for an answer, he continued, "You step into that dressing room in the back." He turned to Hank. "What color you want for those T-shirts?"

"Black and yellow still the colors for Moore Haven Elementary?" At the man's nod, Hank said, "Let's stick with those." He grabbed a six-pack of white socks and plunked them down on the glass counter. "These, too, I reckon."

When Noelle gave her dad such a thunderous look the air practically crackled, Kelly fought the urge to laugh out loud. Honestly, the man had no clue. Knowing there was going to be an explosion if she didn't intervene, she stepped into the space between the father and his child. "Honey," she whispered, pulling the girl aside, "why don't you go look at the cowboy hats while I talk to your dad for a minute?" She pointed to a corner of the store filled with stacks of hats of all kinds.

Once Noelle moved out of earshot, she turned to Hank. Getting involved in his life was exactly what she didn't want to do, but a sense of kinship with a lonely little girl made her want to help. "Don't you think your daughter is old enough to pick out her own clothes?" she asked.

"Nah." Hank shook his head. "You see what she's wearing. If I let her shop on her own, she'll end up lookin' like a buckle bunny at the rodeo."

Kelly stole a quick glance at the child, who had unearthed what had to be the only pink-feathered Stetson in the store. While the girl preened in front of the mirror, she conceded that Hank had a point. Noelle couldn't be left to her own devices. But Hank and the salesman weren't much help, either.

"Okay," she agreed. "I'll help her pick out a few things. There are chairs in front of the dressing rooms. You go sit in one." At the confusion that swam in Hank's eyes, she shook her head. "It's going to take some time," she said slowly. "We'll be along in a little while."

"We're just grabbing a couple of…" Hank glanced over one shoulder to the waiting area. "You sure?"

If there was one thing Kelly understood, it was a girl's need to feel pretty. "If she steps into a pair of jeans she likes first thing in the morning, she'll be a lot more likely to be in a good mood for the rest of her day. You want her to enjoy her time here, don't you?"

Though the sad look Hank aimed at his daughter nearly broke her heart, Kelly quashed her urge to give the man a sympathetic hug. The past was past. She wasn't about to dredge up old feelings that might lead to new hurts. Forcing herself to stay strong, she pointed to the dressing area. "Okay, then. Let's do this."

Though his rounded shoulders told her Hank still didn't quite get it, she gave him credit for trying when he folded his long frame into the chair. Kelly turned away, tamping down a stab of longing while she gathered her wits about her to help Hank's daughter.

At Noelle's side, she lifted the hat from the girl's head. "That's a little too fancy for everyday. We don't want to scare the horses." She feigned horror and gave an exaggerated shiver that brought a smile to the child's lips. "What if we pick out some tops and jeans first. Then, once we know your style, you can find a hat to match."

"I like sparkles," Noelle said shyly.

"What girl doesn't?" Kelly agreed.

Having established some common ground, they forged into the children's section. Before long, they had amassed a pile of glittery shirts and jeans with ornately stitched pockets. Her arms filled, Kelly grabbed a couple of pairs of Wranglers and two long-sleeved tops for herself on their way to the dressing rooms.

"Make sure you try on everything," she told the girl. "I want to see it all."

While Noelle changed into her first outfit, Kelly stepped into a pair of jeans she could just as easily wear running errands as horseback riding. A quick peek in the mirror told her the chignon she'd worn to the attorney's office was too prim and proper for the casual clothes. She tugged at the pins and sent her hair cascading past her shoulders. She worried the blouse might be a bit too snug, but, anxious to see how Noelle had done with her choices, she stepped from behind the curtain. All decked out in sequins and glittery jeans, the little girl beamed up with her first honest smile of the day.

"Those are perfect for you," Kelly declared.

"I like them." Noelle shook her head and laughed

when the beads shimmied. "I like yours, too," she murmured.

"Let's see what your dad thinks, okay?" Her hand on Noelle's shoulder, she turned the girl toward the man in the chair. "What do you say, Hank?"

The rancher's piercing blue eyes honed in on the girl. A crooked smile tugged at the corners of his lips, and the lines around his eyes deepened. "I'd say you both make those clothes look mighty good."

"So, I can keep them?" Noelle asked tentatively.

"Of course." His posture more relaxed than it had been the past few hours, Hank aimed his chin toward the curtain. "Now, don't you have another outfit or two in there?"

Noelle ducked into the changing area. "Wait right there," she ordered, as if she suspected her dad had someplace he'd rather be. "I'll hurry."

Kelly ran her fingers through her hair. Maybe Hank and his daughter were on the right track after all. Not sure who she was trying to convince, she tossed an extra measure of reassurance into the smile she gave her old friend.

But the look Hank focused on her went way beyond the neighborly one she'd expected in return. Her heart stuttered, though she insisted it had nothing to do with the spark of interest she glimpsed in his eyes. Nothing at all to do with the low whistle that whispered across his lips as he took in the shirt and jeans she instantly decided she couldn't live without. No matter how snugly they fit her curves.

THE STIR OF attraction took Hank by surprise. To make matters worse, an admiring whistle passed between his lips before he could clamp them shut. This wasn't what he wanted, he told himself. Not after the last time. Though he was certain his family and friends thought he'd sailed through his high school breakup unscathed, he hadn't. In truth, he still carried the scars of losing both his girlfriend and his *best* friend in one horrible night. Unable to turn to the person he'd always counted on to understand him, he'd poured everything he'd had into bustin' broncs in the rodeo. But getting thrown off a horse and landing butt-first in the dirt had only added to the pain of his broken heart.

Nope, he wouldn't get involved with Kelly again. No matter how well she filled out a work shirt. Or how his pulse leaped when he saw her in that pair of jeans.

He shook his head when she ducked back into the changing room without saying a word. She emerged a few minutes later wearing the same Wranglers with a loose shirt that didn't have quite the same throat-tightening effect. Relieved, he let his guard down, his gaze drifting along with it. But down was no good, either, because the red-soled heels that peeked out from beneath the hem of her jeans only sent his heart into overdrive.

This time, he caught the whistle before it escaped. He'd seen shoes like those before. He thought they were called Lou-something-or-others. Amy had a closet full of them—though he had to admit, hers had never revved his engine in quite the same way.

One thought about his ex-wife, though, was all it took to throw a bucket of cold water on his libido. He remembered all the stupid mistakes he'd made after he and Kelly had called it quits. Mistakes that had led to a marriage on the rebound. Mistakes he was still paying for.

He risked a glance at Kelly, who gave no sign she'd noticed his fleeting interest. Glad they didn't have to *talk* about his momentary lapse, he deliberately turned his focus to the reason he'd brought them to Eli's in the first place…and the one good thing to come out of his ill-fated marriage.

He gave his daughter's next outfit a nod of approval before, with Noelle sandwiched between them, he and Kelly shopped for boots and a hat to complete the child's wardrobe. Whenever he could, he kept his distance, leaving the choice of color and style up to the girls. In the boot aisle, he prepared for a fight over an elegantly stitched pair that cost more than a month's pay. He needn't have worried. Kelly merely pointed to brown ones more suited to ranch work.

"I have a pair of those. They're my absolute favorites," she insisted.

And just like that, his headstrong preteen had to have them, too.

He was pretty sure Noelle tried on every hat in the store before Kelly said a gray felt Stetson complemented her eyes. He wasn't quite sure about all that, but he liked the way Noelle's face glowed beneath the dark brim. The smile she gave him when he told her so warmed his heart. Though his wallet was considerably lighter after he paid for their purchases, it was worth every cent to see delight instead of censure in his child's eyes. "You hungry?" he asked as he carried Noelle's new clothes to the truck, while Kelly lingered behind to pay for her own purchases.

"Yeah, sure," Noelle nodded. In the backseat, she scooped her cell phone into her lap.

Hank hummed as he slid behind the wheel. "We'll swing by Cowboys for burgers," he announced.

"Burgers?"

How such a tiny little slip of a girl could cram so much disdain into one word was beyond him, but Noelle accomplished the task as if she were born to do it.

"They have other stuff," he backpedaled, wondering where he'd gone wrong. "Great barbeque. Steaks, too, though we're throwing some of the Circle P's best on the grill tonight in your honor."

"From cows?" In the rearview mirror, he watched as Noelle's fingers flew over the keys on her cell phone. "You know I'm a vegetarian!"

Hank propped one arm on the seat back. "How long has this been going on?"

"Like, duh, forever. Aren't you supposed to know stuff like that?"

"No-elle." Hating himself for it, he let his voice drop into a lower register. "You ordered fried chicken when I took you out for your birthday."

Noelle's chin jutted forward as she folded her arms across her thin chest. "The whole family went vegetarian to support Grampa after his heart attack."

Well, excuse him for not being in the loop. Except, wasn't rectifying that situation the reason he'd insisted she stay with him instead of going to boarding school? He wondered how his daughter's "no meat" policy would go over with the cooks on the Circle P and frowned. He lived on a cattle ranch, after all. Beef, in one form or another, was served at practically every meal.

Casting about for help, he glanced up to see his own personal cavalry emerge from Eli's in jeans and a new shirt. Confident Kelly would know how to handle this latest quirk in his daughter's personality, he waited until she added her bags to Noelle's before he broached the newest in what was apparently a never-ending series of hurdles.

"Uh, Kel, we have a little problem."

"Whatever it is, can it wait?" She slipped out of her high heels and crossed denim-clad legs. "I'm famished. You can tell me about it over lunch. My treat, since you drove and paid for the gas."

Hank did his best not to stare as she massaged one slender foot. He and Kelly always had been on the same wavelength. It had boggled his mind when they were teens. Twelve years later, it still did.

"Noelle and I were just discussing that very thing. I suggested burgers at Cowboys, but she's not into meat these days. Got any ideas?"

Kelly merely shifted to his daughter. In a tone far less judgmental than the one he'd used, she asked, "Vegan? Or are you more flexible?" At Noelle's confused look, she continued. "Do you eat eggs and dairy? What about seafood?"

"Shrimp are okay, as long as they're fried. Mom makes me drink a glass of milk every morning." Noelle made a face. "I don't like it much."

Kelly tapped one finger against her chin. "Got it. If I remember right, The Clock has the best salads in town. Good burgers, too," she added with a grin.

Before anyone—and by anyone, he meant his prickly daughter—changed their mind, Hank drove to the restaurant. The lunch hour crowd had thinned, and soon they were settled in a roomy booth. The waitress handed them plastic-coated menus that offered a variety of salads and vegetarian dishes. He and Kelly traded amused glances, but neither said a word when Noelle skipped the healthy stuff in favor of mac and cheese and a plate of fries. Determined to get in his daughter's good graces, he dug deep into his pockets for spare change so she could play video games until their food was served.

As she headed off, he turned a decidedly neighborly glance at the woman seated across from him. "Thanks for all your help today, Kelly. I don't know what's gotten into her. She's never been like this before."

"Relax." Kelly squeezed a wedge of lemon over a glass of sweet tea. "She's just pushing your buttons, trying to find out where the limits are. Things will smooth out."

Uncertain, he ran a hand through his hair. "How'd you get so smart about kids?" She was an only child, and it wasn't like she had a lot of nieces or nephews to learn from.

"We fill a lot of entry-level positions with high school students at Palmetto Boots. I don't work with them as much as I did when I was managing a store, but I used to deal with teens all the time." Ice cubes clinked softly against her glass as she swirled a spoon through the tea. "Some of them can get pretty sassy. I gave them a firm hand." She shrugged. "They usually came around."

Hank cupped his hands around his own glass. "Do you think I did the right thing by insisting she come here?" It had only been one day, and he already felt like he'd been ridden hard. Much as he hated to admit it, he wasn't sure how much more he could handle.

Kelly's eyes narrowed. "Don't you want to spend time with her?"

"More than anything." Trusting his one-time friend would understand, he didn't try to hide the wistful quality that seeped into his voice.

Without looking up, Kelly settled her spoon on her napkin. "I was her age when Mom dumped me with Pops."

She'd been such a big part of his life that he'd nearly forgotten she hadn't been around until the fourth grade. "That had to be tough," he acknowledged. "You ever hear from her?"

For an instant, he caught a glimpse of the girl who had once cried on his shoulder. Then Kelly's features straightened. Staring into her glass, she said, "'Bout five years ago, I got an envelope in the mail. Inside was a newspaper clipping about a car crash in New Mexico and a death certificate with her name on it. No note. Nothing else."

"Your grandfather sent it?" At Kelly's nod, he swore softly. "You two never did get along, but that was cruel. Even for him." If she'd been closer instead of clear across the table, he would have put his arm around her and given her a hug. As it was, he had to settle for words that seemed inadequate. "I'm sorry."

Dry-eyed, she finally glanced at him. "Mom made her choices. Pops, too, I guess." They fell silent for a while, each busy with their own thoughts. He glanced into the game nook in time to see his daughter slip another coin into one of the machines. He had three months to get things right with her before her mom took her home again. All too soon, Noelle would be old enough to do whatever she wanted. This visit could be his last chance.

"I'm afraid things will turn out between Noelle and me like they did between you and your grandfather," he admitted at last.

Kelly's head rose. "If you want the kind of relationship Pops and I have, it's simple. Just don't do anything. He certainly didn't even try." Blinking rapidly, she drummed her long, slender fingers on the tabletop. At last, she stilled. "I'm sorry," she said, lifting her hand. "Your relationship with Noelle is none of my business."

Across the room, his daughter guided a mechanical claw through a glass box filled with inexpensive stuffed animals. Kelly had no idea how deep his daughter's resentment went. Or how well he'd earned her low opinion of him.

"Speaking of your grandfather, what went on at the lawyer's office?" he asked, putting aside the topic of his daughter for the moment.

Kelly ran her fingers along the placket of her new shirt. "Turns out that shortly after my grandmother died, Paul added my name to the title of the Bar X."

Powerless against his shock, Hank let his surprise show. "You own the place?"

"There are some legal hoops to jump through, but yeah, basically."

For someone who'd just learned she owned a valuable piece of property, Kelly didn't look happy. In fact, if he was reading the tightness around her mouth right, her grandfather had pulled another fast one on her. He leaned back, trying to fit the puzzle pieces together while he waited for her to tell the rest of the story.

Across from him, she straightened the silverware on her napkin. "The day I turned twenty-one—long after I'd moved away—Pops wrote out a Power of Attorney. It gives me the authority to do whatever I want. With him. With the ranch. With everything on it. Whatever happens next, it's all on me."

"And he never changed it? Never told you?" It was hard to believe, but then, Paul Tompkins had always been a difficult man to understand.

"Never said a word." Her shoulders rose and fell as she took a breath. "Not that he had the chance. We haven't exactly been on speaking terms."

He tried to imagine how he'd feel if the full weight of the Circle P had landed on his shoulders, and failed. Though his family had managed the ranch for two hundred years, the land had—and always would—belong to the Parkers. Staggered by Kelly's news, he asked, "What are you going to do?"

She took a packet of sugar from the caddie and tapped the edge against the table. "I can't stay here," she said at last. "My job, my life, is in Houston."

Hank propped his elbows on the table and cupped his chin in his hands. "You can't leave the livestock to fend for themselves."

"Tell me something I don't already know." Kelly dumped the contents of the packet into her tea. "As near as I can tell, Pops is land rich and cash poor. And since I emptied my savings account to pay for his back taxes, I guess I'm in the same boat."

"Those Brahmans have been a thorn in Ty's side for a long time. If you were to sell them off, he might lend you enough men to round 'em up."

"You think?" Hope flickered in her eyes. "Without the livestock to tend to, I wouldn't need to stick around."

Hank suppressed a flicker of disappointment at her eagerness to put Florida in her rearview. He had no claims on Kelly. What's more, he didn't want any. Their relationship might have burned hotter than a summer wildfire, but the fast-moving flames had scorched his heart. He'd learned his lesson. He'd keep his distance while he extended the same neighborly hand he'd offer any of the other ranchers in the area. "I'll find out who's buying cattle this time of year. Get you a fair price."

"That'd be great, Hank." Kelly sighed, the tiniest bit of tension easing from her lips. "Then I can put the Bar X in the hands of a Realtor and get back to Houston."

Now that had definite possibilities. Hank summoned his most easygoing smile. "You know real estate is my livelihood."

Certain they'd circle back to it, he let the subject drop when their food arrived. Noelle slipped into the booth. Once their drinks had been refreshed, Hank glanced down at a burger half the size of the ones they served at Cowboys. He shrugged, while across the table Noelle scraped aside the toasted croutons that sat atop her macaroni.

"Something wrong?" he asked.

Noelle turned up her nose. "I like the kind that comes in a box."

"O-kay," Hank sighed.

For a few minutes, he concentrated on his food as Noelle gingerly picked at a few bites of macaroni and ate precisely three French fries. As soon as his daughter took a bathroom break, he leaned across the table.

"Let's get down to brass tacks. In order to provide

for your grandfather, you need to get the best possible price for the Bar X. In this economy, that won't be easy, unless you're willing to fix things up a bit."

When Kelly raised her eyebrows, he lifted his hands. "You saw the shape the ranch is in. But I can help. You give me the listing and I'll make the repairs in my spare time." If the Bar X brought as good a price as he thought it would, he'd clear enough to establish a new real estate office once the economy improved and people started buying again. Which would happen. Home ownership was the American dream.

"And in exchange?" Doubt and wariness played across Kelly's face.

"In exchange, you pay for half the supplies. Lend a hand when I need help." He pushed his plate and half-eaten hamburger aside. Getting to know his daughter better—forming a real relationship with her—was the most important thing he'd ever do. Maybe Kelly could help with that, too.

He peered into the face of the woman he'd once loved. Heaven help him. He didn't know which he was more afraid of—that she'd turn down his plan, or that she'd agree to it.

Chapter Four

Hank tapped the toe of his right boot against the floor. He swirled the last of the coffee in his mug and pretended he wasn't counting the minutes as they flew by. Nearly an hour had passed since the last of the ranch hands had polished off their breakfasts and headed to their assigned chores. He should be with them. Should be overseeing the care and feeding of a thousand head of prime Andalusian cattle. Should be riding the fence lines. Should be knocking down that patch of nettles in the north section before the noxious weeds spread. In short, the list of things he should be doing was longer than his arm.

Waiting for a lazy ten-year-old to roll out of bed wasn't on that list.

He rose from his place at the table. Crossing to the screened door, he peered out. Star and Belle stood in the riding ring where he'd left them. The horses stomped their hooves, as eager as he was to get the day started. Hank checked his watch. Eight in the morning. He'd planned to evaluate Noelle's riding skills before he started on his chores. It was too late for that now. He carted his mug to the coffeepot for a refill. When he flipped the handle, a few drops dribbled into the cup.

"No more coffee," he grunted. He glanced toward the counter, where Chris chopped vegetables for tonight's supper.

"Sorry, Mr. Hank." Beneath the young man's knife, a pepper turned into fine green ribbons. "We don't usually keep the pot going during the day when no one's here to drink it."

Hank shook his head. On the busy Circle P Ranch, everyone had a job to do and was hard at it. Everyone except him, apparently. Deciding he'd waited long enough for Noelle to meander into the kitchen, he started toward the hall. The distinctive sound of a new pair of boots striking the stair risers stopped him. Hoping to tap into his daughter's good side—assuming she had one—Hank swallowed an urge to scold her.

"Morning, sunshine," he called when his ten-year-old clomped into the kitchen. He tore his gaze away from the trail of smudge marks she left on the polished cedar floors. "Sleep well?"

Noelle bobbed her head while her shirt's pink sparkles shimmered in the bright sunlight. "I'm hungry. What's for breakfast?"

No surprise there. Not after the previous night, when Her Royal Fussiness had balked at the salad and baked potato Emma had fixed special for her. Hank aimed his chin toward the single place setting he'd laid out on the long trestle table. A box of cereal stood nearby.

"That's all?" Noelle's eyes widened as if he'd suggested she go on a fast. "I smelled pancakes."

"For those, you have to show up when the bell rings." He pointed past the kitchen door to a brass bell mounted on a tall post. The cook gave the rope three sharp tugs to summon ranch hands, guests and family members for meals.

The corners of Noelle's mouth turned down, but her disappointment showed for only a moment before she issued the standard "whatever." Still, Hank had a feeling his daughter would scramble out of bed on time in the future. "I guess I'll have cereal," she said, sounding as if she were doing the world a favor.

"You want orange juice? Milk?"

Noelle poured a generous helping of cornflakes into her bowl. "Milk. For the cereal. Can I have some coffee?"

"Sorry. Fresh out." Hank tapped his empty mug. "Besides, you're too young."

"Mom lets me," Noelle pouted.

"Yeah? I'll ask her next time she calls."

"Don't bother." Noelle's eyes cut to one side. "I only drink Starbucks anyway."

Hank turned away so his daughter wouldn't see his face. Score one for the old man, he told himself. He battled a grin into submission before he turned back to Noelle.

"Soon as you finish eating, we'll head out. Ty ordered a new solar array for one of the water pumps. It'll take most of the day to install it." Instead of the horses, they'd have to take one of the ATVs. Between the late start and the need to keep his daughter entertained, he feared the job could stretch into two days, and put him further behind schedule. "You might want to bring a book or something. Your cell phone's no good out that far."

Noelle froze, her spoon halfway to her mouth. "You have to work?"

She made fresh air, sunshine and long rides in the country sound like a bad thing.

"Ranching is a full-time job. Six, sometimes seven days a week."

"I have to start school Monday, Dad. Who's gonna take me?" A pleading tone crept into her voice. "When will I pick up my uniforms?"

"Uniforms?" He scrubbed one hand along the seam of his jeans. The kids who waited for the bus at the end of the driveway would probably laugh themselves silly at the idea of pleated skirts and button-down collars. "Round here, the dress code is a bit more casual than you're used to."

If he thought that would please his daughter, he was wrong. His little drama queen's mouth widened like a starlet's in a horror movie.

"You can't expect me to wear these—" she gestured to the outfit he'd paid for with hard-earned money "—to school." She shuddered.

"What's wrong with your clothes?" Hank fought an urge to scratch his head.

"Da-ad!" Noelle's spoon dropped into her bowl. The move sent a splatter of milk onto the table. "I can't wear the same outfit to school every other day. The kids will tease me."

"Didn't you bring anything with you?" Hank asked, hoping his daughter's woefully light bag had contained more than it appeared to. "What about what you wore to your old school?"

"Johnston Prep gave us uniforms." Noelle rolled her eyes. "Besides, Mom told me to pack my pajamas, my bathing suits and some shorts. She said you'd take care of everything else. She said you should have plenty of cash now that you aren't giving her money."

Slowly, Hank slid onto the bench across from his daughter. Okay, sure. He'd had his child support payments reduced after the housing market dried up. But from the moment he and Amy had separated right up until Noelle came to live with him, he'd sent every spare penny to her mother each month.

He stared out the window. Despite Noelle's surly attitude, even he knew she couldn't make it through an entire semester on three pairs of jeans and a couple of T-shirts. But he'd already taken a day off to pick his daughter up at the airport. If he took another one, Ty would be within his rights to dock his pay. He racked his brain, searching for a way to be in two places at once.

"Finish your breakfast," he said at last, "and brush your teeth. We'll see if Kelly can take you."

"Honest?" A new interest crossed his daughter's face.

"We'll go ask her as soon as you're ready." Hank rubbed his chin. Taking his daughter shopping would definitely stretch the definition of *"lend a hand when I need it,"* but swinging by the Bar X would give him an excuse to check in on the woman who'd spent the night alone on the ranch.

After wolfing down her cereal, Noelle dashed upstairs. By the time she sped down again, Hank had already turned Belle and Star over to one of the ranch hands along with orders to unsaddle the horses and give them a rubdown. Twenty minutes later, he clenched his teeth to keep them from rattling as his truck bounced along the rutted driveway onto the Bar X. Pulling to a stop, he made a note to have the entry graded and smoothed before he put the ranch on the market.

He scanned the yard, stopping when he spotted Kelly at the clothesline. Dressed in work clothes, her hair coiled under a bandana, she swung a broom with the grace of a major league baseball player. Dust swirled in the air every time she made contact.

"Hey," he called, stepping from the truck.

"Hank. Noelle." Kelly lowered the broom she'd been using to beat a defenseless rug into submission. "What brings you to the Bar X so early?"

Before Hank had a chance to say a word, Noelle blurted, "You have to take me shopping."

"Noelle!" Hank barked a sharp rebuke. "Ms. Kelly doesn't *have* to do anything. We're here to ask her for a favor."

"Sor-ry." Looking more defiant than apologetic, Noelle toed her boot through the dirt.

"What's this about, Hank?"

Kelly pinned him with a look so intense he had to fight to keep his wits about him. Anchoring his thumbs on the pockets of his jeans, he glanced at the barn where the door to the hayloft dangled from its hinges. "I'm here to offer you a trade," he said, forcing nonchalance into his voice. "Noelle needs a few more clothes for school. But if I don't get the solar array repaired in the south section, I won't be able to move cattle onto that grass like I need to. If you could take her shopping and stop by the school on your way—" he wiped a damp palm against one pant leg and nodded toward the barn "—I'll come over this evening and fix that door."

Kelly shifted the broom from one hand to the other. "I was planning to head into town to visit my grandfather at the hospital. As long as you wouldn't mind coming with me?" She turned expectantly to Noelle.

"I won't catch anything, will I?" the girl asked.

"No." An amused smile broke across Kelly's face. "He's not contagious. Just old and hurt. Did you know your daddy probably saved his life by getting him to the hospital the other day?"

The unexpected praise warmed Hank from the inside out. He scuffed a boot through the sand. "I only did what anybody would do," he insisted. Changing the subject, he tugged a lone credit card from his wallet and ballparked a spending allowance. "We're all set then?"

"Let me get this straight." Kelly eyed the plastic without reaching for it. "You want us to shop for an entire school wardrobe. In one day. And spend how much?"

"You just need to buy enough to get her through December," Hank corrected.

"Why?" Thin lines marred Kelly's brow. "What happens then?"

"He gets rid of me, that's what." Noelle whipped out her cell phone, her attention waning.

Hank glared at the preteen, who was doing her best to stir up trouble. "It's not like that, and you know it, Noelle. Your mom will get back from her trip at the end of November. She and I agreed that you'd stay with me till the end of the term."

"Whatever." His daughter shrugged. Her fingers poised over the keypad, she aimed a hopeful look at Kelly. "So, will you take me?"

Hank caught the frown Kelly tossed his way before she turned a smile on his daughter. "I'd be glad to," she said. Taking his credit card, she slipped it into the pocket of her jeans without meeting his eyes.

Suddenly best buddies, the two girls headed for the house while Hank ignored a jealous twinge. More than anything, he wanted to prove he could be a good father to his only child. But he'd made his bed by striking a deal with Kelly. Now he had no choice but to lie in it until he finished his chores for the day. That night, he'd start getting the Bar X into tip-top shape. In another few weeks Kelly would return to Houston, and his life could go back to normal. Wishing someone would deliver that message to his heart, he aimed his boots toward his truck.

OF ALL THE MEN in all the Wranglers in the world, why did this one make her insides quiver like no other? Even as her stomach tightened, Kelly refused to acknowledge the attraction that swirled through her. Keeping things platonic between her and Hank wasn't just the right thing to do. It was the only thing to do. Circumstances might have thrown them together again, but she'd traveled the relationship road with the tall, dark-haired rancher once. And once was enough. She wouldn't, couldn't risk getting hurt like that again.

She shook her head, intent on driving the point home. Her mind got the message. If only it would pass the news along to the rest of her, she'd be fine.

"C'mon inside." She motioned to Noelle, glad the busy day they had planned would prevent her from dwelling on memories of the girl's father. "It won't take me long to get ready, and then we'll be off."

Twenty minutes later, she found Noelle on the front porch.

"What's up?" she asked, noting the preteen's long face.

"My friends have forgotten me. No one is returning my texts." Noelle stared morosely at the cell phone in her lap. "It's not fair. I didn't want to move. Why'd they make me?"

A familiar hollow spot opened in Kelly's chest. She knew what it was like for someone to upend your whole world without warning. Her own mom had done exactly the same thing more times than she could count. What were Hank and his ex thinking, committing to a plan that would bounce Noelle from one end of the state to the other? Didn't either of them care how hard moving back and forth was going to be on their daughter? Her heart went out to the girl.

"I moved around a lot, too, when I was your age." She accepted Noelle's surly nod as a sign of the same kind of nervousness she'd felt before she came to the Bar X.

Noelle spared her a sideways glance. "I bet you never had problems fitting in."

"You'd be wrong about that. I was in the fourth grade when I moved here to live with my grandfather. The school year had already started. I felt lost."

"Did the other kids tease you?"

The shy uncertainty beneath Noelle's usual bravado made Kelly's heart ache. Eager to put the kid at ease, she gave her most comforting smile. "The Circle P might not be the biggest ranch around, but the Parkers and the Judds have roots that go way back. Once the local boys and girls find out you're one of them, they'll accept you. Jimmy and Bree, they'll look out for you, too."

Noelle's mouth quirked to one side. "They're just little."

"Don't let age fool you. Ranch kids stick together."

Kelly let the girl mull that over while they headed for her grandfather's truck. Whatever she'd said must have resonated with Noelle, because the child was on her best behavior from the moment they pulled into the parking lot at Moore Haven Elementary. In the office, they spoke with a matronly secretary who confirmed Noelle's registration and handed her an information packet along with her teacher's name.

"It's a teacher workday, but most of the staff is at a meeting over at the school board," she said at length. "I have to answer the phones or I'd show you to your room. You're welcome to explore on your own if you'd like."

One glance at the nervous child beside her and Kelly decided that was exactly what they should do. She led the way through halls decorated with student artwork. In the corridor outside one of the fifth-grade classrooms, a janitor ran an electric buffer over freshly scrubbed floors. The smell of wax and disinfectant tickled Kelly's nose, while the girl beside her peered through security glass at small desks in neat rows.

She hadn't lied to Noelle, Kelly reminded herself. Not exactly. But she'd never found it easy to walk into a strange classroom. Throw in the fact that her mother's nomadic existence hadn't exactly put studies at the top of her priority list, and Kelly had spent her first few days at Moore Haven wondering if she'd ever fit in. Those feelings had lasted one long, miserable week… until Hank Judd had slid his tray beside hers at lunch. Minutes later, Colt and his younger brothers had joined them. From then on, she'd been accepted. Abandoned by her mom and unloved by her grandfather, she'd finally found friends who had her back. She glanced at the wisp of a child beside her. Didn't she owe it to Hank to help his daughter find her way at Moore Haven, the same way he'd helped her all those years before?

Once Noelle knew how to get from the main entrance to her classroom and from there to the cafeteria, Kelly drove them to a mid-priced department store in nearby Okeechobee. There, with a list of the school's dos and don'ts in hand, she and Noelle spent hours selecting clothes that the child liked and that met the school's requirements for closed-toed shoes and sleeves. When they'd finally assembled an appropriate wardrobe, they headed for the cash register, where Kelly hoped they wouldn't max out Hank's credit card.

"Kelly Tompkins, as I live and breathe. It's been ages! How are you?"

"Fine—" Kelly swept a quick look at the ID tag worn by the clerk behind the counter "—Marie. Just fine." She summoned a big smile for the vaguely familiar woman.

"I heard you were back in town. How's your grandfather? I hope he's doing better. And is this your daughter?" Marie asked, without pausing for answers. She frowned. "No one mentioned you had a child."

"Oh, she's not mine, but we're having such a good time, I almost wish she was." Kelly aimed a smile toward Noelle. She hadn't complained—not even once— over the past two hours as she tried on one outfit after another. "Noelle, Marie and I went to the same high school. Marie, this is Noelle Judd, Hank's daughter. He was tied up at the ranch today, so we're having a girls' day out."

"Oh?" Marie's gaze sharpened as it swung to Noelle and stuck there. "Well, you sure could have fooled me. She's got your eyes, your hair."

Kelly glanced toward the girl and swallowed. The baby she'd lost would only be another couple of years older than Noelle. Would that child have inherited her fair skin and sandy-blond hair? Or would the baby have had Hank's dark hair and blue eyes?

Marie turned to the register. "We're running a special on socks today," she suggested. "Three pairs for five dollars. You want to pick out some to match your outfits, honey?"

Noelle tugged on Kelly's sleeve. "I'll never wear the ones Dad bought."

Hank had meant well, but bulky white cotton didn't exactly make a fashion statement. "I think we can afford a couple of pairs. Just stay where I can see you," Kelly cautioned. She was not going to lose track of the independent preteen.

The instant Noelle reached the display, Marie placed the T-shirt she'd been folding on the countertop. "People 'round here still talk about you and Hank. None of us could figure out why the two of you broke up. Did you catch him with one of the gals from the rodeo?" She leaned forward, a predatory gleam in her eyes.

"Ancient history." Kelly gave her head a firm shake. There was no way she'd confide in Marie. The woman had never been her friend and would probably spread any gossip she gathered to half the town. Kelly cleared her throat and gave the clothes a pointed look. She might as well have saved herself the effort, because Marie didn't budge.

"So, are you and Hank back together?"

"Not a chance." The protest escaped her lips before she could stop it. "I'm only in town because my grandfather's sick. I'm putting the Bar X on the market, and

Hank offered to handle the sale. That's all there is to it." She straightened ever so slightly. "I'm headed back to Houston as soon as possible."

Marie's shoulders rounded. The clerk once again began scanning price tags and folding clothes into bags. "You picked out some nice things," she said, her attention shifting as the prospect for juicy gossip dimmed.

The minute Marie's focus swung to the next customer, Kelly herded her charge toward the door. She eyed the girl who had fallen uncharacteristically silent. "I sure appreciate your going to the hospital with me today. You up for one last stop?" If they hurried, they could still swing by to see her grandfather and make it home to the Bar X before dinner.

"I guess." Wearing a frown, Noelle lowered her bag into the cargo space behind her seat. "Were you and my dad, like, together in high school?"

The conversation was not one Kelly wanted to have with the girl. But she couldn't lie—especially since Noelle had undoubtedly overheard at least part of the conversation with Marie.

"Your dad was my best friend." It was the truth, though for a while there he'd been so much more.

The lines across Noelle's forehead deepened, and her mouth slanted to one side. For a second, Kelly froze, certain the child would press the matter, but Noelle only reached for her earbuds and slid onto the passenger seat.

Kelly took a breath. She'd have to talk to Hank. Much as she didn't want to dredge up old heartaches, his daughter was too curious, too insistent to let the subject drop forever. Which meant she and Hank had to get their story straight before Noelle raised the topic again.

After checking in with the front desk at the hospital,

Kelly steered them through wide corridors to a room where someone had scrawled Paul Tompkins's name on a slate outside the door. Soft snores came from behind a curtain separating the room's two occupants. Propped between pillows, her grandfather slumped in his bed, his body tilted to one side. The thin, hospital-issued gown had slipped down, exposing a sunken chest. Kelly swallowed.

"You okay, Pops?" Gently, she tugged the gown over a wrinkled shoulder that looked too pale compared to her grandfather's suntanned arms and face. Gently tipping his head back against the pillows, she kept her voice low.

The old man's eyes slowly blinked open. "AmGoMa-Nah?"

Kelly bit back a frown when he stared at her as if what he'd said made perfect sense.

"I'm sorry, Pops. I didn't get that." She blotted his damp chin with a tissue from the nightstand. Her grandfather mumbled the same garbled phrase.

"Why's he talking like that?" Noelle clung to the doorjamb with white knuckles.

"His doctor says he had a stroke." Kelly patted her grandfather's shoulder. "But it'll be okay, Pops. We're gonna take good care of you."

"Will he get better?"

Well, he was awake. That had to be a good sign, considering he'd slept through her previous visits. Kelly brushed a strand of white hair off her grandfather's face. "I hope so. He's moving to a rehab center in the morning. His physical therapists will help him learn to speak and use his arm again."

She smoothed a rumpled blanket over the plaster cast. "How's your leg, Pops? Any pain?"

"Can I watch the TV?" Noelle asked. She slid into the hard plastic chair by the door.

"Sure. You'll have to scoot over here next to Pops to hear it, though. The speaker is in the remote." She plucked the device that served double-duty as a call button from the bedside table and held it out.

Noelle glanced at the washed out figure in the bed and sidled closer. "He's not gonna get up or anything, is he?"

Kelly gave her grandfather's arm a squeeze. "You couldn't if you wanted to, could you, Pops?" To Noelle, she added, "The cast on his leg is too heavy. Plus, he's having trouble moving his right arm and leg for now." She tossed out a compassionate smile. "Will you be okay alone with him for a few minutes?" She frowned at an empty water pitcher on the tray at her grandfather's elbow. "Let me fill this," she said, hefting the plastic container, "and find out what time they'll move him tomorrow."

Noelle gave the old man in the bed a final look, then grabbed the remote and started flipping channels. "What do you like, Pops?" she asked. "Soap operas? News? Sitcoms? Not much to choose from, is there?" As if she knew waiting for an answer was pointless, she settled back against her chair.

Kelly lingered at the door until the sounds of a laugh track rose from the tiny speaker before she headed for the nurses' station. There, after a short wait, she spoke with the charge nurse, who reported there'd been little change in her grandfather's condition. Reassured he was doing as well as could be expected, Kelly filled the pitcher and headed back to the room. She paused outside the door when she heard Noelle's soft murmurs.

"He opened the door and the bucket of water spilled on him, see? That's funny, isn't it?"

Her heart thudded when Paul's rheumy eyes followed the movement on the screen.

"Mmmha," he mumbled.

"Whatever." Noelle's go-to phrase had lost its usual sarcastic quality. "Watch what happens next. The guy's gonna slip in the water, and the bucket's gonna come down on his head."

Sure enough, it did, and along with it, Paul gave a garbled response.

Amazed at the first sign of involvement her grandfather had shown in the three days since the stroke, Kelly fought tears. "You're pretty good with him," she said, tiptoeing into the room when the program went to commercial.

Noelle sprang to her feet. "Sure. Whatever." She rubbed her stomach. "I saw a little store in the lobby. Can I have a candy bar?"

Kelly gave the child a squeeze. "You're such good medicine, you've earned it." Eager to see her grandfather's lopsided smile for herself, she turned to buss his cheek. But the eyes that only seconds earlier had focused on the golden-haired child were now drifting shut. Kelly tried to ignore the little voice that whispered he'd turned away from her on purpose. Swallowing, she faced Noelle. "You ready to head out, kiddo?"

"Can we do this again?" Noelle asked a short time later, while she munched on her snack.

"I'd like that," Kelly answered, without hesitation. She had enjoyed spending the day with the child. Besides, she told herself, someone should show an interest in the girl. Because, apparently, Hank had better things to do than spend time with his only child.

INTENDING TO DELIVER a quick report before he headed for the Bar X, Hank poked his head into Ty's office. "The solar array is up and running. I swung by the bunkhouse at Little Lake. Spotted a couple loose boards and a few screens that need replacing, so I sent Josh and two of the men there overnight. No sense waitin' till the trail rides in November to start getting things in shape for our guests." His plan to move on derailed when the owner pushed away from his computer and stretched.

"I sure appreciate the way you're keeping tabs on things. I can't seem to get away from all this paper-work." Ty gestured toward the piles of bills and ads. "Are the men staying busy?"

Hank considered his answer carefully. Though no one slacked off on the Circle P, the ranch had its down times. "It's always a little slower between the summer roundup and late fall." Which might work in Kelly's favor, if and when she asked Ty for his help.

The owner squinted at the calendar. Half the days in September were already crossed out. "Won't be long be-fore things pick up again. Our birding tours are booked solid from Christmas into spring. I've already started a waiting list." In the five years since he'd taken up the reins on the busy South Florida ranch, Ty had focused on diversifying the Circle P's interests. By opening the winter cattle drive to tourists and expanding his wife's tropical flower business, he'd rescued the ranch from near bankruptcy. His newest venture—overnight trail rides at the height of the migratory bird season—could finally put the Circle P's bottom line soundly in the black.

Ty gave the calendar another glance. "Garrett's baby is due next month, isn't it? Have you heard anything from him?"

Hank rolled his shoulders. "I spoke with Mom last week. Arlene's still in the hospital. She's gotta be bored out of her mind." Enforced bed rest and a long hospital stay had accompanied the high-risk pregnancy. "I know she'll be glad when this part's over."

"Oh, but that's just the beginning. At least, that's what they tell me."

The dinner bell sounded, and Hank waited for the final note before he continued. "I'll have the boys move the cattle into the south pasture tomorrow. Should be good grazing there for a month or so."

Ty rose from his desk. "Walk with me to the kitchen?"

"Nah. I'm headed to the Bar X. The door to Tompkins's hayloft is hanging by a prayer. I promised to fix it if Kelly watched Noelle today." Something glinted in his friend's eyes, and Hank paused, uncertainty tugging at him. "You don't mind my doing a few things over there, do you? Kelly's given me the listing. I think I have a buyer for it." He'd contacted all of his old clients about the ranch. Only one—John Jacobs—had shown any interest, but he was flying in to look at the place in a couple of weeks. "He wants everything to be damn near perfect, so I'm trying to fix what's broken."

"What you do in your free time is none of my business." Ty's gaze wavered for a second before it steadied. "Pity you're gonna miss supper, though. Sarah's got a meeting in town tonight, so Jimmy and me are bachin' with the rest of the boys. Chris fixed a Mexican casserole. We're gonna see who can eat the most of it."

Relieved when Ty didn't say anything about him and Kelly, Hank tracked the boss's long strides down the hallway. He'd seen the concern flicker across his friend's face, but honestly, the man had nothing to worry about. He'd help sell his former girlfriend's ranch and earn a big commission in the process. After that, they'd go their separate ways.

Determined to stick to the plan, he crossed the great room to the front door. Stepping onto the porch, he clamped his hat tighter, lest a freshening breeze send it skittering. The northerly wind was a sure sign they were in for a change in the weather, and he made a note to check the forecast before the men headed out in the morning. While a late-season storm might bring a much-appreciated drop in temperature, lightning was dangerous on the flat countryside. And, as long as he managed the Circle P, it was up to him to keep the ranch hands safe. Which meant not sending them out when a storm threatened.

By the time Hank drove his truck onto the Bar X, the golden sun balanced atop a cloud bank at the distant edge of the horizon. Lights in the barn drew him away from the house and, walking across a yard so hard-packed it didn't give grass a chance, he wondered how much he owed Kelly for her spending the day with his daughter. If Noelle had kept her sullen shell wrapped around her, he suspected not even repairing the barn door would be enough. Had he been wrong to insist the child spend the semester with him instead of sending her to boarding school like his ex wanted? He shook his head. Their time together hadn't gotten off to a great start, but things would get better.

Halfway to the barn, he caught the sound of laughter. He paused in the shadows, meaning to stop only long enough to find out what had intrigued his daughter and Kelly.

"He's so tope," Noelle gushed as she brushed Tompkins's mare.

"So, you like him? Or what?" Kelly's tone contained so many questions, Hank didn't need to see her face to know her eyebrows had skyrocketed.

"Well, duh. He's tope. That means he's the best. And he likes me, too. Last time Mia and Shelly and I went to the mall, we ate at the food court. He stopped by our table to talk. My friends said maybe he's going to ask me out."

Ask her out? Hank's back teeth slammed together. At ten, he was pretty sure his daughter ought to be thinking about ponies and multiplication tables, not which boy was the cutest. He started forward, but stopped at Kelly's easygoing manner. Her words drifted over the divider from the next stall.

"Are you allowed to date?"

Noelle's voice dropped so low Hank had to lean in to hear her.

"Mom says I have to wait till I'm fourteen." A stronger gust of wind rattled a shutter against its frame. When his daughter spoke again, the old attitude was back, equal parts self-pity and protest.

"That's so not fair. A lot of my friends have already been kissed. Do you think he'll even remember me when I get back?"

"Well, you said he was a smart boy. He'd be a fool

if he forgot you." Kelly spoke with conviction. "I don't know if I'd be in such a hurry, though. Your dad and his brothers pulled a lot of practical jokes on me when I was your age. Once, they convinced me to sneak out and go snipe hunting in the middle of the night."

"What's a snipe? Did you catch one?"

Hank smiled at Noelle's breathy questions. He'd been quite taken with the new girl in town from the moment Kelly had walked into their fourth-grade classroom, but his brothers would have teased him mercilessly if he'd let it show. That didn't stop him from watching out for her. Take the night of the snipe hunt, for instance. Keeping out of sight, he'd trailed her through the palmetto and scrub oak to keep her safe.

"It was a trick. There's no such thing as a snipe," Kelly said solemnly. "You'll be better off if you forget about boys till you're fifteen or sixteen."

Hank stifled a groan. He and Kelly hadn't been much more than that when things had gotten serious between them. He resettled his Stetson and wished he was the one having the heart-to-heart with Noelle. He'd tell her to wait until she was twenty, at least, to fall in love. Maybe then she'd avoid the mistakes he'd made and the heartache that, twelve years later, he still felt whenever he thought about the girl who'd dumped him. Rubbing his thumb over the tender spot in the center of his chest, he pushed away from the side of the barn he'd been holding up. He let his boots ring against the cedar flooring as he moved farther into the wide aisle between the stalls.

"Noelle? Kelly?" he called, as if he hadn't spent the past five minutes eavesdropping.

"We're back here," Kelly called out.

"Is it time to go already?" Noelle's tone switched to the slightly bored, mostly exasperated one she used whenever Hank put in an appearance.

"Not yet. I'm here to fulfill my part of the bargain. I brought my tools and a new hinge." He turned to Kelly. "Mind if I get started?"

Kelly glanced up as if she could see through the flooring above them to the opening to the hayloft. The lips he'd once loved to kiss straightened into a thin line. "You're going to need help supporting that door. I'm finished with Rusty." She gave the gelding a final swipe with her brush.

Hank peered over the Dutch door into a stall where, if tufts of knotted hair were any indication, someone had spent far too much time talking and not enough tending to her chores. "Looks like you've got some more work to do on Lady," he told Noelle. "When you finish with her, refill all the water troughs. If you need more to do, you can muck out the stalls till we're done."

"I wanted to text my friends." Noelle's hands landed at her waist. "They're waiting to hear from me."

Hank rocked back on his bootheels. He wondered if he'd ever get used to his daughter's smart mouth. Or if she'd ever learn to temper it. Before he had a chance to repeat himself, Kelly interrupted.

"I'm sure your dad has a really good reason for wanting you to stay in the barn. Right, Hank?"

When Kelly stared at him with those big green eyes, he had no choice but to soften his stance. He cleared his throat and ripped his gaze from her. "The barn door weighs more than I do. It probably won't fall, but if it did, I'd hate for anything to happen to you."

Noelle's focus shifted from Kelly to Hank and back

again. Apparently their united front presented his daughter with too great a challenge, and her shoulders drooped. She picked up the curry brush and ran it through the horse's coarse hair. "Okay," she said, though her long-suffering sigh let everyone know she wasn't happy with the situation.

Hank eyed Noelle for a long minute. Phrases such as *"I love you"* and *"I'm so glad you're here"* tickled his tongue, but his daughter only shrugged a thin shoulder and turned away from him, murmuring softly to the horse while she brushed. Would he ever earn a place in the girl's heart? He spun on one heel, crossed to the ladder and began to climb, determined to focus on tasks he could handle rather than on problems he couldn't solve. But as he stepped onto the rough floorboards in the loft, the smell of sweet hay tickled his nose, reminding him of times when he and Kelly had snuck off to be alone in a place much like this one.

He cleared his throat. "I apologize for her behavior," he said, concentrating on his daughter so he wouldn't concentrate on Kelly. "I hope she wasn't like that all day."

"We actually had a good time together." Kelly studied him. "Make sure you ask about her clothes. She picked out some nice things."

Clothes. He fought the urge to slap his forehead. "Guess I shoulda asked that first, huh? I got a little distracted hearing her spill her guts to you about her boyfriend."

"You heard that, did you?"

"Some of it. She should be talking about stuff like that with me, not with you."

"Maybe if you spent more time with her, she would,"

Kelly shot back. "If Pops had done that with me, maybe we wouldn't be in the spot we're in right now."

Hank held up his hands. Being more involved in his daughter's life was exactly why he'd insisted she come to the Circle P, but every time he tried, he seemed to make matters worse. To hide his consternation, he drew on his strengths. He was better at fixing things than he was at fixing relationships.

As he suspected, the bottom hinge had broken, leaving the heavy wooden door dangling from a lone strip of metal at the top. Certain it wouldn't support the weight much longer, Hank tossed a rope over a rafter and gave an end to Kelly to hold. Then, fighting a growing wind, he muscled the door closed and threaded the loose end of the rope through the handle. Once he tied it off, he turned to Kelly.

"Keep tension on it," he said.

She did, and he turned to the job at hand. He'd barely managed to tap the new hinge into place before a strong gust of wind rattled the barn. With a loud, grinding squeak, the door slipped off the chocks he'd wedged under it and swung wide. Kelly stumbled forward, the rope pulling her toward a gaping hole and a three-story plunge to the ground.

"Let go!" Hank called.

Unable or unwilling to do so, she clung to her end of the rope. Her boots slipped on the slick hay. Hank sprang to his feet, grabbing her as she slid past.

Suddenly, his arms were filled with familiar curves that belonged to the living, breathing woman of his dreams. For several seconds after the wind died down, he held her tight. Inhaled her scent. Breathed into her hair. Having Kelly in his arms again was enough to make a thinking man forget his own name.

Chapter Five

One second, she was sliding across the hay, hurtling toward certain injury. Or worse. The next, her body had slammed into a wall of muscle. Solid male muscle.

Kelly grabbed hold and held on tight. Her feet skidded to a halt. The rope slipped from her fingers.

Gradually, awareness seeped into her consciousness. Hank snugged her against his broad chest. His strong arms wrapped around her waist. Thighs as thick and solid as tree trunks pressed against her, sending a wave of delicious warmth coursing through her. Her head had landed on his shoulder, instinctively finding the tender hollow below his collarbone. She listened as his pulse picked up speed.

She stirred, intending to back away, intending to put some distance between them. Instead, her fingers clung to the downy softness of his T-shirt. She took a steadying breath, but rather than gaining strength, she sagged against him as her head filled with a familiar spicy, musky scent.

Memories of their last months together crowded forward. Back then, just one tantalizing whiff of Hank had been enough to drive her to distraction. Of course, they'd been teens then. Inexperienced. Awkward. Easily swayed by raging hormones.

But there was nothing awkward about the man who held her now. Nothing inexperienced about him, either.

Somehow, her hands found purchase on his wide chest. All thought of pushing away from him faded as she traced lazy circles across his T-shirt. His deep groan echoed through her midsection. His grip on her tightened until she tilted her head, wanting to see the same need reflected in his dark eyes. It was, and when his lips came crashing down on hers, it felt like the most natural thing in the world to open to him. Her mind reeled as long-buried wants and desires surged to the surface. Sighing into him, she sifted her fingers through his thick hair, which brushed the collar of his shirt. She curled her hand around his neck, drawing him closer, deepening the kiss. For a long minute, she gave herself to the touch, the taste, the feel of him. His grip on her waist eased in response, his long fingers climbing her ribs. As one thumb brushed her breast, she gasped.

"Hank, I…"

"Shh, baby," he whispered. "For a moment there, I thought I'd lost you."

But he had lost her. Long ago. And giving into whatever was going on between them now couldn't happen. She wouldn't let it happen.

She slid her hands down to his muscular chest, and, as much as she wanted to stay right where she was, shoved at the arms that held her.

"Dad? Kelly? You okay?"

She snapped back to reality the instant Noelle's voice rose through the ladder opening. Hank's hands dropped from her sides. The fine sandpaper of a five-o'clock shadow brushed her cheek as he stumbled back.

"We're fine," he called, his voice strained. "The door got away from us for a minute, but we'll have it back where it's supposed to be in a jiff."

Staring into Hank's blue eyes, Kelly knew he meant putting more than a barn door back in place. Regret rushed in on the cool breeze that filled the space between them. She pushed it down, insisting the interruption only reinforced a decision she'd reached on her own. A single kiss had nearly turned her brain to mush, nearly made her forget how Hank had let her down when she'd needed him most. What would happen if they let things go further?

Stifling the urge to find out, she took another step away from Hank. The best thing—the only thing—to do was to put some distance between them. She couldn't let her old flame distract her. Her focus had to remain on taking care of her grandfather. On returning to Houston. To the big promotion she'd worked so hard to achieve. That meant getting the Bar X ready to sell while keeping things strictly professional between her and Hank. Which certainly meant no trading kisses with the man. Even if kissing Hank was like returning after a long trip to find an explosion of yellow ribbons and "Welcome Home" signs littering the front yard.

She brushed her fingers over kiss-warmed lips and inhaled a breath of air that smelled more of hay and impending rain than of Hank and the past they'd shared. "Let's do this," she said, snagging the loose end of the rope.

Unwilling to risk a repeat performance of the near accident—or her weak-kneed reaction to Hank's touch—she drew the line taut. She backed farther into the hayloft, wrapping the rope securely around a post. Braced for another rogue gust of wind, she nodded to Hank. If the breeze or her feelings kicked up again, she'd be ready to resist them both.

She thought she saw the same mixed emotions shimmering in Hank's eyes as he turned away from her. But he bent once again to the task of replacing the broken hinge without saying a word. This time, the work proceeded without a hitch, and ten minutes later, they climbed down the ladder, the moment they'd shared apparently forgotten.

Hank never once sent a meaningful glance her way as he loaded Noelle into his truck and sped into the deepening night. Kelly watched the vehicle's taillights until they disappeared around a bend in the road.

Trudging into the house moments later, she admitted that Hank's embrace, his kiss, had stirred feelings she thought she'd long since overcome. But, as much as she pretended she didn't care anymore, she still missed having Hank in her life. Loneliness swept over her, and she prepared herself for a restless night. Sure enough, after two hours of trying to count sheep and losing track every time her thoughts veered into forbidden territory, she finally hit on something that would take her mind off the tall rancher and put it where it should be—on her grandfather.

She slipped out of bed and into a pair of work jeans. Then, broom, mop and cleaning products in hand, she systematically worked her way through the house. By the time the sun rose over the cow pasture, she had brushed every cobweb from the corners, wiped inch-thick dust from bookshelves and knick-knacks. She had swept, washed and vacuumed until her back ached and her arms were too heavy to lift so much as a feather duster. Her energy spent, she finally collapsed into bed. Only moments later, her cell phone woke her.

"Hello." What time was it? She squeezed her eyes tight to block out the sunshine.

"Kelly. Randall here. How are things with your grandfather?"

The unmistakably deep-throated growl of the VP of Sales at Palmetto Boots cut through the fog in her sleep-deprived brain. She swung her feet over the side of the bed and straightened, thanking all the stars in heaven that her boss had opted for an old-fashioned phone call rather than his usual Skype session.

"He's holding his own." She waited. She knew better than to think the man had called to discuss her grandfather's health.

"Good. Good to hear." Randall Palmetto cleared his throat and got right down to business. "I wanted to be the first to congratulate you on landing the Ivey's account. They faxed the contracts to us late last night. Everyone here is pretty excited about it."

"Really?" Kelly quickly drove the disbelief from her voice. Her boss did not kid around. Eager to hear the details, she leaned forward. "Were there any last-minute snags? Any negotiating points?"

"No. They accepted all our terms. All your terms," he corrected.

"When do they want their first shipment?" She held her breath. A new customer could take months to reach a decision, and then expect next-day delivery. But ramping up for the chain would take time. Filling such big orders would involve every department in the company—from the tanners who supplied the leather right down to the stockmen who loaded the shipping pallets.

Paper rustled as Randall turned pages. "Looks like we have some time with this one. Delivery is scheduled for December first. That should put us on their shelves in time for holiday shopping."

"Perfect." A lead time of two and a half months was tight but doable. Best of all, it allowed her to attend to her grandfather's business and still be back in time to handle the orders. Picturing exquisite boots under Christmas trees all across the country, Kelly smiled. She waited to hear how her hard work would be rewarded. Landing the big account meant a significant boost to Palmetto Boots's bottom line. She crossed her fingers, hoping it also meant she'd finally get the corner office she'd been working toward ever since she signed on with the company.

"Everyone recognizes the effort you've put into this contract, and we want you to run point on it. This is your baby."

Kelly could practically see her name etched on a glass door.

"Since this is your first major account," Randall continued, "I'll be watching very closely to see how you handle it. This is your chance to prove you can deal with the pressures we expect of our top employees here at Palmetto Boots."

Another chance to prove herself? Hadn't she been doing that from the time she sold her first pair of boots? She'd consistently worked longer hours than any other employee. As a manager, she'd turned her first store into the top producer in its region by overseeing every detail. Later, she'd hit higher sales quotas than any other regional manager. Yet, here she was, being asked to jump through yet another hoop before getting the corner office she deserved. Disappointment knifed through her. Would she ever be accepted into the Palmetto Boots family?

"Yes, sir. I understand," she murmured, swallowing the bitter news like a dutiful child. So it would take another year to earn the recognition she was due. She'd manage it.

"Now, I know you're dealing with some important family matters, but how soon *can* we expect you back in the office? We'll want to get the ball rolling on this account as soon as possible."

"Ten days. Two weeks at the most. I just need to make arrangements for my grandfather's long-term care and handle a few financial matters. Meantime, I can do a lot of the work via email," she said, eager to show she was up to any challenge.

The news added to the urgency of getting her grandfather's affairs settled, but she knew meeting her deadline wouldn't be easy. She had to sell the herd and the ranch. The sooner the better.

But could she count on Hank to come through for her this time? Or would he let her down as he'd done in the past? She drew in a shaky breath. With so much to do and so little time to accomplish it, she really had no choice.

Reluctantly, she picked up the phone and dialed the number for the Circle P ranch.

"THAT SHOULD DO IT," Hank muttered. He powered the engine down. Once he had planted both boots on solid ground, he slammed the tractor's cover shut and grabbed a rag. Wiping grease from his hands, he crossed the yard. He allowed himself a tight smile when his heels struck the front porch steps he'd repaired earlier that afternoon. Though the Bar X was far from perfect, he was making progress. With just a little bit of luck, John Jacobs would fall in love with the place and, soon after, Hank would bank a big commission from selling the ranch.

Unless he'd blown it with Kelly.

He shook his head. What had gotten into him? He'd been up half the night kicking himself for kissing her. The other half, he'd tossed and turned, wishing he'd done it again. And more. He might have spent the last dozen years trying to forget her, but he had to face the truth—he'd never been able to completely erase his first love from his mind. After the kiss they'd shared in the barn the night before, he wasn't sure he ever would.

With a single glance at the young girl sitting in the front porch swing, he pulled hard on the reins of his wandering thoughts. He might have given Kelly another chance…if his heart was the only thing at risk. Trouble was, it wasn't. He had his daughter to think of. His relationship with her had to retain top billing. Even if she hadn't bothered to look up the whole time he'd been standing in front of her.

"Hey, Noelle." He scuffed his foot. When a few paint chips flaked off the cedar boards, he added painting the porch to his list of necessary repairs. "Time to put that away and take a ride out to the pasture with me."

Noelle looked up from her cell phone. "I thought it was gonna take hours to fix the tractor."

"Turned out, it only needed some new spark plugs. Now that it's fixed, we've got cows to tend to." The

Bar X cattle would surely starve to death on the sparse grass. Although ranchers usually saved their supplemental feed for the winter, these cows needed it now. "C'mon and help me." When Noelle still didn't budge, he reached into a regrettably light bag of parental tricks. "I'll let you drive the tractor," he added.

For a moment he was afraid she'd turn him down. After all, what was a tractor ride to a city girl? Instead he saw a rare glimmer of excitement on Noelle's face, one of only a few in the five days since he picked her up at the airport.

"Honest?"

"Your feet won't reach the pedals, but yeah, you can steer once we get out of the yard."

Memories tickled the back of his throat. He saw himself sitting in his dad's lap, his hands on the tractor's wheel while his father worked the pedals. He couldn't have been more than three or four at the time.… Blinking hard, he swallowed. He was getting a heck of a late start with Noelle, but he had to make things right between them before she hit her teens and he lost his chance.

Unable to find the words to tell her how he felt, and half-afraid she'd laugh at him for the effort, he settled for clamping a hand on her shoulder as they crossed the yard to the barn. They climbed onto the tractor's wide seat, where he balanced Noelle on one knee. White smoke filled the air when he fired up the machine. A short time later, with Noelle at the wheel, they bumped over rough ground. When they came to the first gate, Hank let the engine idle.

"Let me show you how we handle these. Then, next time we come to one, you can do it on your own."

He braced for a world-class protest, but Noelle surprised him by scrambling down from the seat to walk by his side through the weeds. Something slithered across the path ahead, and Hank put his arm out, stopping his daughter.

"Always watch where you put your feet," he warned. He pointed to a wavy line in the dirt. "Most of the snakes around here are harmless, and your boots offer some protection. Still, it pays to watch out."

"I know all about snakes," Noelle boasted. "Last year, a man from the zoo brought a bunch of them to our school. I got to hold a rattlesnake. The other kids were too scared."

Hank slowly shook his head. There were some images he could live the rest of his life without seeing. His little girl handling a poisonous viper was one of them. "Those probably had been milked so they didn't have any venom." *He hoped.* "The ones out here won't be. We'll do our best to avoid them."

A loop of chain held the gate fast to a fence post. He slipped it free. Swinging the barrier wide, he wedged it in the grass. They returned to the tractor and he drove it through the opening.

"It's important that we always close up behind us," he explained, as they retraced their steps to loop the chain over the post again. "We wouldn't want the cattle to get into an area that's just been fertilized or sprayed. It wouldn't be good for them." Not that it would be a problem on the Bar X, where no one had done either.

"Where are they? The cows, I mean?" Noelle looked about as if she expected one to emerge from behind the nearest palmetto bush.

"Most of 'em are over that away." He aimed a thumb in the general direction they were headed.

At the next gate, Noelle scrambled down from the tractor before he said a word. Hank drove through and waited until she climbed back aboard. They repeated the process twice before they made it to an enclosure filled with bales of hay and grass wrapped in thick plastic.

Hank glanced over one shoulder at the closed gate behind them. Just as he expected, several head of Brahman wandered toward them on the other side of the fence. He pointed to a calf racing across the field to join the others. "Look at that little fella go. He knows something's up and doesn't want to miss out."

While Noelle watched the gathering herd, Hank levered the tractor blade. He scooped up the first bale and raised the arm into the carrying position. The load slowly sank to the ground, and he frowned. Hank jumped off the tractor, his boots sinking into the soft dirt, but when his daughter started to join him, he held out a hand. "You sit here while I see what's wrong, okay?"

For the first time since they left the ranch house, Noelle protested. "But, Dad, I want to help."

Hank hesitated. As much as he longed to have her at his side, he didn't think his little fashionista would appreciate getting grease on her new clothes. "Trust me," he said softly. Though the girl's expression turned sullen, he grabbed a wrench from the storage box behind the seat. Leaning over the couplings for the hydraulic lines, he spotted a small leak and bent to tighten the fitting. A stream of thick fluid shot out at him, and he jumped back. Not that it did any good. Despite his quick movement, dark goo splattered his shirt, his pants, his boots.

Noelle's laughter rang out, and Hank swallowed the curse that had sprung to his lips. He wiped dark oil from his arms and flung it into the grass, a move that earned him another of Noelle's precious chuckles. He bent again, this time managing to tighten the loose bolt without getting doused with another spray.

Hank stuck the wrench in his back pocket. Once they got back to the barn he'd have to give the system a complete overhaul, but the temporary fix should hold long enough to finish today's task. Babying the tractor along, he removed two bales of silage from the storage area and split them open. Bellowing and lowing, hungry cattle gathered on the other side of the fence as the air ripened with the heavy, beerlike scent of fermented grass.

"Listen to them." Hank shook his head. "They'd gorge themselves on this stuff if we let 'em." He tossed the words over his shoulder as he strode toward the gate alone. Swinging it wide, he waited until the last of the cows passed through before he headed back to the tractor.

"Dad, what about the little one?" Noelle asked when he slid onto the seat beside her. She pointed toward the calf they'd watched run across the field. "The other cows won't let him eat."

Hank eyed the smallest of the gray Brahmans. "He's a feisty little fella. He'll figure it out," he offered reassuringly.

They watched as the youngster ran up and down the line of feeding cattle without finding a place of his own. Finally, he nosed in between two of the heifers. The calf took a bite, snorted and backed out as quickly as he'd come. He sneezed twice before lapping his mouth with his long tongue. Hank was certain if cows could smile, this one would be wearing a broad grin. The next time he plunged in, the calf stayed put.

"Dad, why's everything so brown here?" Noelle asked on the way back to the house.

Hank swept a glance over thin, brittle ground cover that stretched to the horizon. "Ranching is hard work. At the Circle P, we have a whole crew to help out. Kelly's grandfather was trying to do everything by himself."

Noelle's small face scrunched. "How come?"

"I'm not sure," Hank said. Paul Tompkins had always been the cantankerous sort, but whether he'd fired his crew or they'd left because he couldn't afford to pay them, the end result was still the same.

"He's a funny old guy," Noelle continued. "He shouldn't have to work so hard."

"It's a shame no one noticed how bad things had gotten before now." Hank swallowed. His dad would have, if he'd been alive. Seth Judd had always made it his business to know what was happening on the nearby ranches. Swearing to follow in his father's bootsteps, he turned to his daughter.

"Round here, neighbors count on one another to pitch in when someone gets sick," he pointed out. "That's what we're doing now. Helping Kelly and her grandfather out of a jam."

They turned into the yard just as the dinner bell rang. Hank patted his stomach.

"You ready to eat? Kelly said she was fixing veggie lasagna for supper." Which wasn't what he would have chosen—not by a long shot—though he wasn't about to put a damper on his time with Noelle by mentioning it.

"I'm pretty hungry."

Warmth spread through his chest when Noelle rubbed her belly the way he had done. After maneuvering the tractor into place beside the barn with only the smallest bit of help, she turned to him. "Dad—and I mean this in the nicest way—are you going inside like that? You, um, stink."

Hank chortled. "I do, do I? That's what happens when you get sprayed with hydraulic fluid." He pretended to lunge at her, backing off when she giggled and shied away. Sobering, he glanced down. "Point taken. I guess I'd better wash up. You want to head in and tell Kelly I'll be along in a minute?"

He smiled as she ran off, her long, thin legs eating up the ground between the barn and the house. Watching her go, he sent up a fervent wish that their time feeding the cattle had marked a change in his daughter's attitude toward him, toward her stay on the Circle P. He knew she'd love it on the ranch once she gave it a chance. More than that, though, he needed to prove he could be more than an absentee dad, that he could be a real parent to the child he hardly knew. The kind of parent his father had been for him.

He took off his Stetson and slapped it against the side of the barn. A few drops of dark oil splattered to the ground. His soggy shirt required more attention, and he crossed to the watering trough where he stripped down to his jeans. But a good scrubbing with soap and water only spread the stains across the once-white cotton. He wrung the shirt nearly dry and set it aside while he washed up as well as he could.

Water dripped from his hair and ran in rivulets down his chest by the time he finished. He looked around for something to dry off with just as the screen door to the house slapped shut. His pulse quickened as he spied the slim blonde coming down the porch stairs, her arms full.

"Thought you could use these." Kelly handed him a towel and what looked like one of her dad's old shirts.

"Much obliged," he answered, glad he no longer faced the prospect of sitting at her table in clothes that smelled like a machine shop. Though, considering the glint of appreciation he'd caught in Kelly's eyes, going bare-chested didn't seem like a bad alternative. He straightened, subtly stretching his arms and puffing out his chest the way he'd done when they were children.

But those days were long behind them. With maturity came an entirely different reaction than the giggles his posturing had earned him when they were school kids. Instead, a slight flush spread up Kelly's neck and across her face at his lighthearted antics. She never had been able to hide her attraction to him. His body responded the way it always had whenever she'd gotten that dreamy look he'd once taken for granted. When the tip of her tongue darted out to lick her lower lip, he nearly groaned.

He took a single step toward her, wanting, needing, to wrap his arms around her. Desire played across her features, and he knew she felt the same way he did. For one long second, he even thought she'd close the gap between them.

And then what?

Not so long ago, he'd decided to keep his distance from this woman. The one who could make him forget his own name with one come-hither look. He struggled to recall the hell she'd put him through when she'd called things off between them. Hadn't he sworn he'd never let himself be that vulnerable again? Was he honestly considering giving the two of them another chance? He had to keep her at arm's length, but he was afraid he couldn't.

His indecision must have shown on his face, because Kelly's gaze wavered. She tugged her lower lip between her teeth and stumbled back a step.

"Um, this is a bad idea," she whispered, as much to herself as to him. "My boss called this morning," she said, edging away. "I need to be back in Houston within two weeks. This—" she wagged a finger between them "—isn't part of the game plan."

Hank wrenched his gaze from the slender blonde. *Two weeks.* She was leaving. Again. This time he guessed he should be thankful. At least she'd done him the courtesy of giving him notice.

"There's nothing going on between us," he ground out. Nothing but the few sparks he was determined to smother before they turned into a raging fire. Turning his back on her, he shrugged into a shirt better suited to a shorter, thinner man. "We've had our time together. Neither one of us wants a repeat performance." At the lie, a slow, uneven breath seeped through his lips, and he faced her again.

"Sounds like we're on the same page." Relief mingled with regret on Kelly's face. Her expression cleared as she raised her head, her shoulders straightening. "Dinner's on the table. I'll see you inside."

He kept his boots planted in the sandy soil while she made a hasty retreat. Knowing she'd look over her shoulder at him, he turned away, his emotions roiling. The best thing was to keep as far away from Kelly as he could. No matter how much his arms ached to hold her.

Fortunately, Noelle insisted on rehashing every detail of their ride to the pasture while they ate. His conversation with Kelly limited to polite requests for the salt or the butter, Hank was secretly relieved to have his daughter's chatter fill the empty spaces. His stomach even unclenched enough to let him enjoy a few mouthfuls of lasagna, which was surprisingly good despite its meatlessness. Afterward, as Kelly walked them to his truck, Hank did his best to maintain a businesslike demeanor.

"So, what's next?" Kelly asked, while Noelle retrieved her cell phone from the swing on the front porch. "For the ranch," she added.

"I reached out to some of my clients in Tallahassee. One of them, John Jacobs, is interested. He'll be down this way sometime soon. He said he'd stop by to take a look at the place. If that doesn't work out, I'll find another buyer." Hank put as much reassurance as he could into his voice. Truth was, he'd spent hours contacting every single person on his old client list. Only Jacobs had shown any interest, and he wanted the land as a long-term investment. "Meanwhile, we need to get the cattle moved to a fresh pasture," Hank said.

Kelly's hair swung from side to side. "If I'm going to leave in two weeks, I'll need to sell them off. As soon as possible."

"You know you won't get the best price for 'em." The Brahmans had grown thin on Tompkins's patchy grass. Hank ran a finger under his hat brim, thinking. "If we can find someone willing to expand their herd, that might be the best answer to your problem. But you'll need help roundin' 'em up. That's a week's worth of work."

Kelly brushed her hair over one shoulder. "Guess it's time I talk to Ty." She glanced to one side. "Pops would probably skin me alive if he knew I was asking for help from the Circle P, but I'd love to see the hard feelings between our families put to rest."

Hank paused. He knew Ty felt the same way, but it wasn't his place to speak for the owner. "C'mon over to the Circle P tomorrow afternoon," he suggested. "I'll let Ty know you're coming."

Returning from the house, Noelle blurted, "But, Da-ad. You promised to take me riding tomorrow." A scowl marred her features.

Hank grinned at his daughter. "Tomorrow's Sunday. I have the day off. We'll have the whole afternoon together before Kelly gets there."

On the way to the car, Hank couldn't help it. His thoughts kept darting in different directions, to places he didn't want them to go. Though their time in the fields had given him hope he was making progress with Noelle, he couldn't deny the feeling that there was something missing from his life. What would it be like to come in from tending fence lines and have someone bring him a towel and a fresh shirt while he washed away the worst of the day's grime? Would he ever sit down to supper with his daughter and someone special? Someone exactly like Kelly?

Whoa now, he told himself. Those days were long gone. He and Kelly had had their chance. Their dream had died. There was no going back to what they'd had before. For now, he was only here to help her get rid of the ranch that—back when they were young and foolish—he'd thought might one day be their home.

Chapter Six

"At my old school, I didn't have to clean the stalls. I just called the stables, and the groomsman got everything ready for me. I didn't have to stay after, either. Sometimes I did, 'cause I liked to brush the horses. Their noses are so soft. But everybody else let the stable hands do it."

Hank sipped air. No doubt about it, his daughter had led a pampered existence. As long as his real estate business had thrived, he'd been able to give her every luxury—from a private school with its own fancy riding academy to the latest in electronic gadgetry. But after he'd been forced to close his office and his dad had died, he'd realized how shallow that life had been. There were more important things than expensive clothes and designer backpacks. Things like relationships.

If only Noelle would stop fighting him every step of the way, he might have a chance at building one with her.

"We do the same thing here." Hank paused before he added, "For our paying guests." Neither he nor his daughter qualified for the star treatment.

"Well, I don't like mucking. It's dirty, and horse poop stinks. Why can't the ranch hands do it for us?" Noelle propped one hand on her waist and held the rake at arm's length.

Hank sighed. He guessed it was too much to hope that yesterday's change of heart would carry into today. Ever since she'd finally rolled out of bed that morning—though, to be precise, it had been nearly noon before she put in an appearance—his daughter had challenged every decision he'd made. By mid-afternoon he was down to his last nerve. Which she was doing her best to fray. He swallowed a growl and tried again.

"In case you hadn't noticed, Noelle, I *am* a ranch hand. Same as the other men who work here."

"Mom said you're the manager. Why can't you just tell everyone else to do the hard stuff?"

"The best managers lead by example. Besides, I like the hard stuff." He scooped manure and tossed it into the wheelbarrow. "I like the feeling I get when I spread new hay in a freshly raked stall. I know the horses are healthier and happier because I've taken care of them."

"But—"

"Enough, Noelle." Hank let his voice drop into a no-nonsense register he'd resisted using with her. He'd given the girl extra leeway, knowing it couldn't be easy for her to adjust to a new home, a new school, a new parent. He resettled his Stetson. Maybe the time had come to rein in his balky child the same way he'd calm a stubborn calf. He sure hoped so, 'cause he'd flat run out of patience with Her Grumpiness.

With no other options, he propped his shovel against the stall. Hefting the handles of the wheelbarrow, he trundled it toward the dung heap behind the barn. As he passed the open Dutch door where Noelle dawdled, he stopped long enough to give his daughter a final piece of advice.

"On a ranch, there are some jobs we don't hand off to anyone else. If you want to ride this afternoon, you'll muck the stall and saddle your own horse. After we finish, you'll give Belle a good brushing, make sure she's fed and watered. You'll either straighten up or spend the afternoon in your room…without your phone. The choice is yours. Makes no difference to me which one you choose."

Her expression hardened, but the protest Noelle might have offered died when Hank followed up with a look just stern enough to get his point across. He leaned into the wheelbarrow to get it moving again. Trundling it outside, he handled the waste and paused to get his breath. Who knew dealing with a ten-year-old would rip his heart to shreds a dozen times a day? He wiped sweat from his forehead and shuddered to think what life would be like once Noelle hit her teens.

With that stomach-clenching thought, he squared his shoulders and headed back into the barn. He allowed himself a single glance into Noelle's stall on his way to grab a load of fresh hay. His lips twisted into a wry smile when he spotted his daughter—red-faced and apparently holding her breath—while she raked horse droppings onto a shovel. He waited until he was out of sight before he let his smile widen.

Maybe he should have taken a page out of Kelly's employee manual earlier.

And there she was, back in his thoughts again. The other female who had nearly taken over his life. His chest warmed when he imagined telling Kelly about this latest skirmish with his daughter. But instead of letting his imagination wander, Hank deliberately steered his thoughts in another direction. He and Kelly had reached an agreement. They'd made a pact. He'd help her with the Bar X and earn a big commission in the process. That was as far as things would go. It was what both of them wanted.

Yeah, you keep telling yourself that, and maybe one day you'll believe it.

He recognized the lie even when he was trying to shove it down his own throat. He had to be honest. He'd never be able to stick Kelly in a box labeled The One That Got Away and forget about her. Not until they resolved things between them. Not until he knew why. Why she'd called it quits and walked away when he was making plans for their future together. Sure, they'd gotten pregnant. He'd be the first to admit he'd acted like a stupid teenager when she first gave him the news. He hadn't handled the miscarriage any better. But, jeez, he'd been seventeen. Was she going to hold that against him forever?

Sticking a strand of fresh straw in his mouth, he propped his shoulders against the wall of the barn. He tipped his hat low over his eyes and let his mind drift. Kelly was the only one who had the answers. He had to come up with the best way to get her to share them with him.

He wasn't sure how long he stood there, lost in thought, before he noticed the soft sobs. Aware the barn had grown eerily quiet, he felt his breath catch in his throat. *Noelle.* The image of Paul Tompkins lying on the barn floor roared into his consciousness, and he swore. How would he ever forgive himself if his daughter had gotten hurt while he was off daydreaming?

He rushed to the stall where he'd last seen her. His heart skipped a beat when he spotted her standing on a bed of fresh hay. He ran a quick look over her thin torso while he checked for signs of blood or injury. Nothing. Still, she was crying, so something had to be wrong. Had he been too tough on her? That had to be it. He crossed the stall and wrapped his arms around her quaking shoulders.

"Hey, there. What's going on? Are you upset 'cause I said you had to clean the stall?"

"It's not that." Noelle scuffed a boot through what had to be four bales of straw.

Hank clamped his lips shut before a comment about wastefulness had a chance to escape. If not the chores, what had reduced his daughter to tears? There had to be a reason. He gave his forehead a mental smack. "Do you miss your mom?"

"Not really." Noelle sniffed, though she didn't pull away. "She was sending me to boarding school so she could go off on her stupid cruise, remember?"

He might not know much about women, but he'd been around them enough to know this was a good time to shut up and listen. Even if the woman in question hadn't yet reached her teens.

Noelle scrubbed at her eyes. "She was never around much. Before Granddad's heart attack, she stayed busy with her charities and committees and stuff. I had dinner most times by myself or with Imelda, our housekeeper." She brightened the tiniest bit. "Mom and I text back and forth every day though. She's having a good time on the cruise. She said to say 'Hi' to you."

Listening to his daughter try to put a favorable spin on a tough situation, Hank felt his chest tighten. It sounded as if he wasn't the only one whose priorities had been out of whack. He was late to the party and, heaven knew, he had a lot to make up for, but he was going to do his best. He hugged his daughter closer, determined to give her what she needed most of all—his time.

"So, if you're not sad because of your mom, why are you standing in the middle of the barn crying?" he asked softly.

Noelle nudged a pile of blankets and leather with one boot. "Stupid thing's too heavy. I can't put it on Belle."

Hank's gaze traveled from the gentle mare down to the Western saddle he'd slung over the low partition between the stalls earlier that morning. The thing probably weighed half as much as his daughter did. How Noelle had even managed to get it down without hurting herself was a mystery. A girl as slight as she was wouldn't stand a chance of hefting that saddle onto a mare who stood fifteen hands high.

"Hey, now." An unfamiliar tightness made his voice gruff. "Guess that's a mighty big job for a little bit like you."

"I know how to saddle a horse." Noelle toed one stirrup. "This one's a lot heavier than the ones we used at school."

"How 'bout we do this together? I'll lift. You buckle. That sound like a good deal?"

"Will you still let me ride?" Noelle peered at him through tear-filled eyes. She chewed a fingernail. "You said I had to do it all by myself."

"Yeah, but..." Hank's voice trailed off. "Look," he said, when he got it back again. "I'm new at this parenting thing. I'm gonna make mistakes. This is one of them. And I'm sorry."

Noelle's slim arm crept around his waist. "I'm sorry too, Dad. I promise I'll do better."

He swallowed a lump and blinked his damp eyes. "Let's get to it, then."

After positioning the saddle on Belle's back, he watched while Noelle finished getting the horse ready to ride. Once he'd double-checked the billet straps, he stepped aside. He'd chosen the mare for her gentle disposition, and sure enough, she followed easily when Noelle led the way to the riding ring next to the barn. At the entrance to the tack room, they both stopped.

"Do I have to wear a helmet?"

Though Noelle had a stubborn streak, not even her hard head would protect her if she landed in the dirt. Hank fought an urge to wrap her in cotton batting to keep her safe. Instead, he struggled to remember that his dad had managed to raise five sons without losing his mind worrying about them. Surely, he could survive one little girl. He took a breath and tugged on the brim of Noelle's Stetson.

"Most cowboys don't wear 'em unless they're practicing for competition, but I can get you one if you'd like." There were a few helmets hanging in the tack room for the boys who rodeoed.

Noelle shrugged. "I'll be fine. I haven't fallen since I was five."

Hank's stomach plummeted at the thought of his girl taking a tumble. "Were you hurt?"

Despite Noelle's noncommittal shrug, guilt struck a new blow low in his belly. Had he really been so self-absorbed back then he hadn't known, or cared, that she'd fallen? He flexed his shoulders, adjusting to the new weight. What was done was done. He couldn't change the past. But he was definitely going to be more involved in his daughter's future.

"Need a leg up?" He pointed to a wooden platform some of their guests preferred to use. "There's a mounting block over there."

"I think I can do it." Noelle gamely stuck one foot in the stirrup. Though she could barely reach the pommel, she grabbed hold. Leather creaked as she hauled herself into the saddle.

"Good job. How're the stirrups?" he asked when she'd squared herself. He eyed the way her boots fit in the cups. Though he hadn't been too far off when he'd guessed her length, he let the strap out another notch. "Better?" he asked.

Noelle clutched the reins in two hands. She barely blinked down at him. "It feels weird. My legs are too far apart. My weight's off."

Hank chewed the inside of his cheek. His daughter had probably learned to ride English-style at her school. Western-style riding was easier, but it might take her a little while to adjust.

"So, here's what we're gonna do. Today is just practice. I'm going to have you ride around in the ring. Walk first. Then trot. Maybe take a low jump or two. We'll see how you handle yourself. Once you show me you know what you're doing, we'll go for a trail ride after school one day this week."

"Don't worry, Dad. I got this." Noelle split the reins. Her elbows tucked in at her sides, her hands low against Belle's neck, she attempted to pull the horse's head down, while at the same time urging it forward.

The well-mannered mare pawed the ground, but remained in place.

"Ugh!" Noelle expelled a frustrated breath. "What's wrong with her? Why won't she do what I want?"

"Relax," Hank coached. He eased the thin leather strands from his daughter's tight grip and threaded them through one palm. "Riding Western's a bit different from what you're used to, that's all. When you pull her chin down the way you're doing, she thinks you want her to back up. Hold the reins looselike. In one hand. We're usually working cattle and want to keep our strongest hand free for our rope. Or sometimes our hat." He swept his from his head and brushed it against his leg with a teasing "Get along, Little Doggies."

Noelle barely smiled when Belle shook her head and blew air. "My riding instructor says everyone should ride English," she insisted. "I'm very good at it."

"I'm sure you are," Hank said, as agreeably as he could. "And that's fine for an afternoon ride. But cowboys are on horseback from sunup to sundown, so our saddle has to be comfortable—for us and for the horse." He tapped Noelle's saddle. "This one's longer and wider to spread the weight more evenly over the horse's back." He ran a soothing hand down Belle's neck. "Give it a try," he said. "I'm sure you'll love it."

Over the next hour, though, Hank's certainty shriveled like grass during the dry season. He eyed the girl, who sat so stiff he'd swear someone had replaced her spine with a ramrod. For the umpteenth time, he reminded her to hold the reins in one hand. Just as she'd done every other time, she ignored him. Without using her knees, she urged the horse to go faster. The instant Belle broke into an easy jog, Noelle rose in her stirrups. Confused, the mare blew air...and immediately settled into a plodding walk, exactly as she'd done the last dozen times Noelle had attempted to post.

Beyond the riding circle, a horse loped toward the Circle P on the drive from the main road. Dust rose behind the lone rider. Recognizing Kelly's sleek form atop a familiar quarter horse, Hank climbed down from his seat on the top rail. He looked from his red-faced daughter to an increasingly balky mare. He didn't know which he felt the sorriest for, but he had to put an end to the situation. For all their sakes.

"That's enough for today," he called, just as Kelly thundered into the yard.

"Yeehaw!" She brought the grey gelding to an impressive dirt-spraying halt. "I'd forgotten how good it feels to ride with the sun at your back and the breeze in your face." Flushed and windblown, she slid easily from the saddle before Hank could offer to help her. "Hey, Noelle. You look mighty fine on that mare."

Rather than return the greeting, Noelle averted her eyes. With a nod to the girl who looked as if she might burst into tears any second, Kelly slipped the reins over the gelding's head and led him to the corral where Hank stood.

"What's up with the princess?" she whispered.

Hank brushed the brim of his hat in greeting before, his voice low, he answered, "She can't seem to get the hang of the way we do things."

From her perch atop Belle, Noelle piped, "Everyone should ride English. It's the only proper way to ride."

"It looks pretty, I'll give you that." Kelly's lips pursed. "But riding Western sure makes barrel racing a whole lot easier."

Noelle's chin lifted. "You rode in the rodeo?" she asked, her voice filled with wonder.

"I chased a few cans in the Junior Division." Kelly nodded. "Along with your dad and his brothers. We had a blast."

That month of Saturdays when they would all gather in the barn before daybreak, load the horses and gear, and head out to the rodeo, had been some of the best days of his life. With his dad at the wheel and Kelly beside him on the backseat, he used to pray for faraway competitions just so he could hold her close during the long drive. Once they reached the arena, she'd cheered for him while he'd won one gold buckle after another. She'd been a good barrel racer, too, taking home the prize in her division as often as not. And then, one Saturday, she hadn't shown up by the time they had to leave.

He'd bitten the dust in every event that day and come home a loser with empty pockets. Kelly's news—that she was late and scared—hadn't cheered him up one wit.

"You think I could try?" Noelle's hope-filled question drifted across the riding ring.

Hank hesitated. Too bad life didn't come with a re-ride. He'd use his to go back to that day and reassure Kelly everything would be all right.

"Dad?"

He tore his gaze off Kelly. "I don't see why not." He spun his finger in a circle. "You want to give it another go?"

In the ring, Noelle shifted the reins to her left hand. Her posture relaxed the tiniest bit as she clucked to Belle. "C'mon now, gal." She touched her heels to the mare's sides, laughing when the horse broke into an easy lope.

Hank grinned down at Kelly. Here, he'd been fussing with Noelle for the better part of an hour, and all it took was one suggestion from his former girlfriend to turn his daughter around. "Thanks for that," he whispered.

"Glad to help out." Kelly turned to him, a teasing light in her green eyes. "You think you could rustle up a couple of cans?"

Hank removed his hat and ran a hand through his hair. Though the barrels they'd used as kids were long gone, he was pretty sure he could find something that would do.

"Set 'em up for me, won't you? I have to talk with Ty now, but maybe after I finish, we could give Noelle a little demonstration."

"I'd be glad to." For one long minute, Hank watched Kelly saunter toward the house.

"Hey, Dad, look at me. I'm doing it!" Noelle called from the ring.

Another day, another time, he and Kelly would have a heart-to-heart about their past, but there was no changing it. No do-overs. For now, he had to focus on the present and the girl who circled the ring as if she'd been riding Western all her life.

KELLY SPARED A single glance over her shoulder at Hank and his daughter. Ancient sorrow whispered through her chest, stirring the hurt she'd dealt with every day for more than a decade. She put one protective hand over her belly.

She'd done the right thing by calling it off with Hank in high school. Even now, looking back with the perspective of a dozen years, there was only so much she could forgive. Granted, neither of them had planned on getting pregnant—what teenagers did? But Hank had moved so quickly from stunned disbelief to anger, she'd had to ask herself if she really knew him at all. Then, when she'd lost the baby—their baby—his cold indifference had only proven what she already knew, that he wasn't the person she thought he was.

Judging from Hank's troubled relationship with Noelle, he hadn't changed a bit. He had married on the rebound, and divorced soon after. He'd handed all the responsibility—and the joys—of parenthood off to his ex-wife. Though he had a large, loving family willing to pitch in whenever he needed help, he'd all but ignored his little girl. Kelly winced, thinking of all the milestones he must have missed. Noelle's first word, her first step, her first day at school.

She ran a hand over the end of her ponytail. He hadn't been involved when it was easy. How much harder would it have been for him to be a part of *their* child's life? Between them, they hadn't even had two nickels to rub together when she'd gotten pregnant at seventeen. They'd never have been able to give their child the toys, the advantages Noelle took for granted.

But if Hank had stood by her instead of turning his back on her…

Her grandfather might still have tossed her to the curb like yesterday's trash, but Hank would have been there to catch her. He would've put a simple gold ring on her finger. Instead of bumming around on the rodeo circuit, he would've gone to work for his dad after graduation. They would have moved into one of the dozen small houses on the Circle P. She'd have sewn curtains for the windows, painted the nursery, created bookcases out of wood and concrete blocks. Best of all, when the leaves began to change and the first bird arrived on its annual fall migration, she'd have laid their child in the same cradle Hank's parents had used for all five of their sons.

And they'd have loved each other. Wouldn't that have been enough?

In her dreams she sometimes still pictured Hank coming home after a day of riding fence lines or cutting hay. Saw him lifting their baby into the air, giving their child a ride on his broad shoulders. As their child grew older, they'd roughhouse on the lawn, hold sock battles in the living room. He'd read bedtime stories, tuck their little one in at night and turn out the lights. Then, she and Hank would curl up together on the couch, where she'd doze on his shoulder while he whispered sweet words into her ear. When they called it a night and went to bed, they would make love. Slow and easy or fast and furious, she wouldn't care as long as they were together.

If her dreams had come true, would she have been happy? Deliriously so, she admitted. Regret coated the back of her throat, and she swallowed. Sometimes life didn't turn out the way you wanted it to. As a young girl, she'd dreamed of home and family, but as she matured she'd traded those dreams for ones that were far more practical. While her career might never fill her arms with babies, she'd worked hard, pulled herself up by her bootstraps. She'd built a good life for herself, a life she enjoyed. Soon, she'd have the big office and the six-figure income that would prove, once and for all, how far she'd come. Better yet, the next big promotion guaranteed her acceptance into the Palmetto Boots family. The sooner she got back to her life in Houston, the better, she told herself.

She squared her shoulders as her boots struck the first of the wide stairs. The shaded porch offered a cool respite from the heat, and she stepped onto it. Taking a moment, she drank in the scent of the vibrant blooms that hung in evenly placed pots along the eaves. The flowers made a stunning addition to the ranch, and eager to see what other changes Ty and his wife had brought to the Circle P, she reached for the doorknob.

At the last second, she hesitated. Would she be welcome? As a child, she'd raced through those doors completely unaware of the ill feelings between their families. By the time she'd reached her teens, she'd learned to tune out her grandfather's rants about the neighbors while she kept her own friendship with them a secret. Back then, the Parkers and the Judds had accepted her the same way they accepted all their sons' friends.

But, in the years she'd been away, the Parkers had probably spent a lot more money on weed control than they would have if her grandfather had taken better care of his own land. She'd seen the Bar X's poorly maintained fences and knew they caused more headaches for the people who worked on the Circle P. Suddenly uncertain of the reception she'd receive, she took a step back and knocked. She barely had time to gather her thoughts before the door opened.

"Ty Parker," she said, offering her best smile to the grownup version of her childhood friend. The owner of the Circle P had filled out what was once a lanky frame. When a guarded smile replaced the teasing grin he'd worn as a child, she added, "I appreciate your seeing me like this."

Ty swung the door wide. "Welcome to the Circle P," he said, his tone formal. "I was sorry to hear about your grandfather. How's he doing?"

"'Bout as well as can be expected, I guess. They moved him to the rehab center over in Okeechobee. It makes for a bit of a drive to go see him, but he's getting good care." With effort, she stopped babbling.

Ty's lips softened into a sympathetic smile. He stuck one hand in the pocket of his jeans. "I can't exactly say we've been on good terms, but no one wanted to see anything like this happen. You'll let us know if there's anything we can do to help, won't you?"

Kelly gulped, hoping he was as anxious as she was to put an end to the ill will that existed between their families. She drew in strength along with her next breath. "That's why I'm here, Ty. To make things right between us…and to ask for your help."

From somewhere deeper in the house, a door slammed, a dog barked. Childish laughter erupted from the other side of the great room and echoed off the polished hardwood floors. The sound of running feet added to the sudden din. Fearing her words had gotten lost in all the noise, Kelly opened her mouth to repeat them, just as a towheaded boy and a girl with dark curls burst into the room. The boy skidded to a stop at Ty's side.

"Me 'n Bree're going outside, Dad. We're gonna play in the barn."

Creases around Ty's eyes deepened as he frowned down at the boy. "Whoa now, partner. Mind your manners. Say *hello* to our guest."

"Sorry." An abashed look crossed the face of the

boy. He struck out his hand. "Jimmy Parker. Pleased to meet you."

Kelly extended a hand to Ty's adopted son. "Pleased to meet you, too," she said.

"I'm Bree Shane—ow!" Rubbing her ribs, the tiny girl glared at her playmate.

"Judd," hissed the boy who'd jabbed her with his elbow.

"Oooh, sorry. I mis'membered." Her frown flipped over on itself. "Bree Judd." Beneath a halo of curls Colt's stepdaughter offered up a saucy smile.

Her heart melting, Kelly blinked at Ty. "Must be nice having a new crop of kids around the ranch. It's been a few years, hasn't it?"

Memories danced in the big rancher's eyes. "Too long," he admitted. His expression softened as he stared down at his son. "You climb into that hayloft again, there'll be no dessert for a week." When Jimmy swore they were only going to visit some new pups, Ty shrugged. "C'mon back to the office. We can talk there without being interrupted."

He led the way across the glossy cedar floors they used to skid across in their socks when they were a little older than Jimmy and Bree. In the far corner of the great room, a leather couch and chairs had replaced the worn upholstered furniture where their gang had watched TV on rainy summer afternoons. A few more photographs had been added to the gallery of Parker and Judd pictures, but the place hadn't changed much more in the years since her last visit.

Once Ty settled behind the large, paper-strewn desk in the office and Kelly took her place in a comfortable guest chair, she got straight down to business. "Ty, we both know the Tompkinses and the Parkers have a long, acrimonious history. I'm hoping between the two of us we can put an end to the hard times and forge a better future for both ranches."

A healthy dose of skepticism raised Ty's eyebrows as he leaned forward to prop his elbows on the desk. "I'm mighty glad to hear you say that, Kelly, but I'm not sure your grandfather would feel the same way."

"I had a long talk with his therapists this morning." Kelly sighed. Much as she had hoped the doctors were wrong, Paul's speech was still garbled, and one side of his body was completely paralyzed. "Given the extent of the damage, there's not much hope for improvement."

Honest sympathy shaded Ty's face. "How are you holding up?"

Kelly hid her emotions behind a brave smile. Ty might have been an old friend, but he didn't need to know how much she'd hoped to patch things up with her grandfather. Fate had apparently denied her that opportunity. Determined to achieve one good thing during her trip home, she said the words she'd rehearsed that morning.

"First, I want to thank you for sending your crew over to move my cattle to a new pasture this week. Between that and the silage Hank opened up, I can keep the herd fed. At least for a little while."

Ty motioned her thanks aside. "I was glad to do it. Things on the Circle P slow down after the spring roundup. We won't get too busy again till fall, when the trail rides get going. Helping out gave the men something to do besides sittin' around watchin' the grass grow."

"Well, thanks just the same. I know those Brahmans

have created big problems for you. I want you to know Hank's helping me locate a buyer for them."

The lines across Ty's brow deepened. "There's no need to sell your cattle on my account. While it's true I've never been overly fond of Brahmans, you have the right to raise them…as long as you maintain the fences between our properties."

"There's more to it than that, as I'm sure Hank has told you." Not that she'd fault him for talking out of school.

Ty shrugged his shoulders. "Nah, he didn't say much. Just that your grandfather probably wasn't going to ranch anymore. And that you'd be heading back to Houston soon. Why? Is there more to the story I need to know?"

"I wouldn't say *need,* exactly." Wondering why Hank hadn't filled Ty in, she took a deep breath. "Pops has always been…" *Mule-headed. Vengeful.* She paused, unable to choose the right word.

"Difficult?" Ty prompted.

"Yeah, let's go with that." She guessed it was as good a description as any. Her grandfather had always been one to hold a grudge. He'd never forgiven the Parkers or the Judds following the crash that killed her grandmother. Not that they'd had anything to do with it. Granny had been on her way home after doing the neighborly thing—delivering a covered-dish supper the week Doris Judd had given birth to twins—when her car had veered off the road. She'd died instantly. It had been a terrible accident, certainly no one's fault. But Pops had never recovered from the loss. Lately, though, the way he'd neglected the Bar X went far beyond irrational.

"It's no secret Pops has been acting stranger than normal lately. He ran up charges all over town. Pretty much let the ranch fall into ruin. All the ranch hands either quit or left on their own. If I hadn't paid the property tax, we'd have lost the place altogether."

Ty whistled. "I knew the old man was slipping. But I had no idea things had gotten so bad."

"Nobody did." She waved a hand through the air to let Ty know she didn't blame him. "It took me a while to figure out what happened. But after talking with Pops's doctors, I realized this wasn't his first stroke. The tests showed he'd had a series of small ones. I think the doctors called 'em TIAs. Over time, the damage adds up. It probably explains why he's been acting the way he has."

She leaned into her chair, crossed one booted foot over the other. "The upshot is, I need the money I'll clear by selling the herd."

Some of the stiffness eased out of Ty's shoulders. "I'm glad you're not selling out just for me. But let's think about this a minute. If you hang on to them till winter, your cattle will bring a better price."

She shook her head. "I'm afraid Pops let things go too far. The pastures need weed kill and fertilizer I can't afford. Besides, I have to put the ranch on the market."

"So, you're really letting go of your heritage?" Ty's gaze drifted to the window overlooking land that had been in his family for more than four generations.

Kelly took a minute. Ever since she'd come back to the Bar X, she'd made a habit of carrying her coffee out to the front porch each morning. Soaking in the peace and quiet while the sun rose in the east, watching the brilliant gold clouds gradually turning pink and then white as the sun rose higher in the huge sky—it was the best part of the day. She loved hearing the distant *mrrruuh* from the cattle, the first bird calls of the day. This morning, she'd gawked at a family of deer that had wandered across the lawn while she'd sat, sipping.

The Bar X had been in her family nearly as long as there'd been settlers in Florida. So, yeah, she wished she could hang on to it. But, as her grandfather's only asset, it wasn't hers to keep. She had to sell the land to pay for his care. A shudder passed through her.

"Don't have much choice," she admitted slowly. "I emptied my savings account to pay the tax bill. Can't get a mortgage. The banks won't lend money to a long-distance rancher with no track record. Medical bills are already starting to mount. I have to sell."

"Sounds like you've given this considerable thought." Ty tapped a pencil against his desk. "What can I do to help?"

Here came the tricky part, the part that left her beholden to a neighbor. "Once Hank finds a buyer for the herd, I'm going to need some help rounding up the cattle. If you could see your way clear to lending me your crew when the time comes—at a fair price, of course—I'd sure appreciate it."

"A roundup?" Ty swiveled to stare at a large wall calendar crowded with notes and appointments. He frowned.

Kelly slumped in her chair, certain she had asked too much of her childhood friend.

"Assuming we do this soon, I can free up some of the crew," Ty said at last. His gaze softened as he turned to her. "But keep your money in your pocket. It's no good here."

Being neighborly was one thing, but she wouldn't accept the man's charity. "Nothing?" Kelly straightened, bristling. "I insist on paying a fair price."

Ty held up a hand. "It's good to see you've inherited some of your grandfather's spirit," he said, his brown eyes serious. "Look, I'm not doing this out of the goodness of my heart. Not entirely." He propped his chin in one hand. "I can't tell you how tired I am of shelling out good money on a pregnant heifer, only to have her drop a mixed-breed calf I end up selling for a loss."

Another rancher might not care so much about preserving the bloodlines of his cattle. But the Parkers' herd traced its lineage to the cows that arrived with the first Spanish explorers. Still, Ty's offer was far too generous. Her grandfather would tan her hide if she accepted help she couldn't pay for. Then again, hadn't she come to the Circle P in part to put an end to the tension between the ranches?

She rose to her feet, her hand extended. "I'm much obliged, Ty," she said, swallowing her pride. "You or anyone on the Circle P need a new pair of boots, let me know. I'll make you a deal you can't refuse."

Her hand in Ty's warm grip, they shook, putting an end to a feud that had lasted longer than either of them could remember.

As she started to leave, the door behind her creaked open. A breath of fresh hay and spice wafted into the room. A warm feeling spread through her before Ty's focus even swung from her to the new arrival.

"Hope you don't mind my interrupting, but as long as you're both here," came the voice that haunted her dreams at night. "I just got off the phone with the new owner of the Barlowe place."

Kelly smiled. The locals would refer to the ranch as

the Barlowe place until they decided the new owners were staying put. In, say, a generation or two.

"He's looking to get into the cattle business and jumped at the chance to buy your whole herd, Kelly. Offered to match the market price. Best part is, he doesn't mind if the cows are a bit on the scrawny side. He's got plenty of good grass, and isn't in any hurry to send 'em to market."

The news was almost too good to be true, and one glance into Hank's blue eyes told her there was a catch. "But…?" she asked.

"But he needs to take delivery by a week from Sunday. I can't find anyone to haul them on such short notice. So…" Hank glanced at Ty.

"So we'll have to have a cattle drive," the two men said in unison. They stared at her, their faces filled with eager anticipation.

Kelly pictured herself riding by Hank's side on a two-day cattle drive over Florida's pristine countryside. Her heart thrilled to the idea of long days in the saddle, sharing picnic lunches in the shade of tall pines. Of sleeping under the stars with only the lowing cattle and the soft scurry of night critters to break the silence. It sounded like a little slice of heaven, a fitting way to end her time on the ranch. Except…

Her gaze shifted away from Ty. Her pulse ratcheted upward when she thought of sitting beside Hank at the campfire each night. Of the thin canvas tents they'd sleep in. The tents with walls that couldn't keep out a mosquito, much less separate two people who were as drawn to each other as they were. Her mouth went dry, and she swallowed.

"I'm in," she said, not at all sure she was strong enough to resist slipping into Hank's arms once they were alone in the wilderness.

Chapter Seven

From his seat atop Star, Hank studied the buzzards that looped in lazy circles over the pond. His gaze dropped to the wide-eyed calf that had wandered into trouble and now stood, mired in muck, twenty feet from shore. Sammy barked at the weaner, his four paws planted at the water's edge. The cow dog spun, chased his tail and yipped again. The calf strained at the rope, but didn't budge. The little one's mother could probably tempt her baby out of the water, but Hank scanned the endless stretch of patchy grass beyond the pond without spotting her.

Not that he'd exactly call a hundred-pound calf "little."

He tipped his hat, mopped sweat from his brow. Leave it to him to be on his own when he found a Brahman stuck in a mudhole. He hadn't planned it this way. No, when he'd pictured how his day might go, he'd imagined Kelly at his side. They'd talk while they flushed cattle from their hiding spots in the bushes. With the cow dogs' help, they'd herd the stragglers toward the southern-most pasture on the Bar X in preparation for a weekend cattle drive. If he was lucky, he'd steal a kiss or two from Kelly along the way.

But not a single light had glowed from the windows of the Bar X when he and his crew had ridden through that morning. More disappointed than he had any right to be, he'd barked orders at the ranch hands like an old cow dog. The first chance they'd gotten, the boys had put as much distance between him and them as possible. They'd headed in different directions, each intent on scouring every copse for silver-sided cows. Which had left him alone to deal with a calf that had gotten itself into a jam.

Slowly, Hank backed Star another step. The rope grew taut. The horse's bridle jangled. The noose around the calf's neck tightened a skosh but, legs splayed, the young one stood his ground in the murky water.

"Damn." There was nothing else to do but go in after the weaner. For a half second, Hank considered moving on without her, but he couldn't leave her where she was. Sooner or later, the calf would tire and drown. That was, if the gators didn't finish her off first.

He studied the clumps of algae without spotting a single pair of eyes staring back at him from the surface. Which didn't mean sloshing into the pond was a good idea. Gators held their breath for hours when they wanted to. A big one could be lying on the bottom, still as a log, waiting for the right moment to strike. Hank scoured the muddy slope down to the water. The tension in his shoulders eased a bit when all he saw were the tracks of small animals. Grumbling about the general stupidity of calves, he dismounted.

He let loose a few choice words as he waded well past the point where silty water rushed over the tops of his boots. The late-summer sun would dry his clothes. His boots, though, were an entirely different matter.

After a plunge in the pond, they'd be a soggy mess for the rest of the day. Yet he knew better than to remove them. They did, after all, offer some protection against things that slithered around in the muck. And things with big teeth.

"Hey now, baby girl. It's gonna be okay. We'll get you out of here. Easy does it."

Reaching the calf, Hank patted its head. He waited until it stopped bawling before, muscles straining, he lifted it free of the muck. The calf in his arms, he sloshed through the thigh-high water to the shore, where he carefully lowered the youngster. Exhausted after spending who knew how long in the water, the calf stood on trembling legs. Hank's heart thudded. The corners of his mouth lifted. He glanced down at himself. Above the waist, he was a sweat-soaked mess. Below his belt, mud and pond scum dripped from his Wranglers. His socks squished inside his boots. His chest expanded as he drew in a deep breath of sun-kissed air.

This, he told himself, this was what he was made for. Ranching ran in his blood, as sure as it had in his father's and his father's before him. Selling real estate had its good points, no doubt. But rescuing a tiny calf from a watery grave gave him more pure enjoyment than he'd ever gotten from closing a deal or banking a commission check.

"Aw, if only I could make a living at it, I'd stay," he muttered to the calf, which hadn't run off as he'd expected. Suspecting the poor thing would never make the long walk to join the rest of the herd, Hank re-coiled his rope. He looped it over Star's pommel. A minute later, his muscles sang as he lifted the calf onto the horse and climbed on behind it. His arms filled with the bawling heifer, he clucked to Star.

"There, there," he murmured, stroking the short gray spikes atop the calf's head. "We'll get you to your mama soon enough."

He whistled to the dog, which lay in the shade of the one palmetto bush within shouting distance. Sammy sprang to his feet. Tail wagging, he trotted closer, only to plop down on his rear and whine. Canting his head, he stared up through intelligent brown eyes.

"Yeah, I hear ya. Calves ain't supposed to be up here. So sue me." Hank touched his heels to Star's sides.

Sammy fell in alongside as the big gelding moved forward. A fifteen-minute ride took them to the field where Hank had opened another tube of silage to supplement grass the gathering herd would certainly overgraze in a matter of days. The calf stirred, anxious to find its mother, and he gently lowered the baby to the ground. He grinned as it frolicked off, apparently fully recovered from its recent dunking.

Wishing he could say the same for himself, he brushed a mix of muck and slime from his jeans. He chose a spot beneath a lone tree, where he toed off his boots. Sure enough, water gurgled out when he upended them. He settled for wringing his socks as dry as he could get them before he stepped into the leather, which would no doubt never be the same again.

A breeze whispered through the branches overhead. A motor rumbled in the distance, and Hank smiled at the sight of an ATV cutting through the tall grass. Leaving Star to fend for himself, he strolled over as Kelly stepped from the vehicle.

"Missed ya this morning." He touched the brim of his work Stetson.

Kelly nodded. "The rehab center called a little after two. Pops had a bad night, but he finally settled down."

"Sorry to hear that." Hank's heart lurched when she ran a hand over her face. Despite missing a night's sleep, she looked a sight better than he did at the moment.

"What ya got there?" he asked, just as she bent into the little truck bed. He gave up the fight and ran his gaze over a figure that curved in all the right spots. The woman could rock a pair of Wranglers and boots, he'd give her that much.

"Thought you and the boys might like a treat. It's not much, just store-bought."

A hunger for something sweet flared within him when Kelly held up trays loaded with what looked like the entire bakery section of the local market. Only, what he wanted wasn't made of sugar and flour. To give his hands something to do besides reaching for Kelly, he grabbed the walkie-talkie he'd stuffed into Star's saddle bag. He keyed the rest of the crew.

"Break time, boys. Meet us under the shade tree. Miss Kelly's brought snacks."

He waited as, one by one, the hands responded. By the time the last one reported in, he spied three of the riders cutting across the flat prairie.

Hank lowered himself onto the bottom step of the ATV. "You got any liquid soap? I'm not sure I should handle food with these." He held up his grimy hands.

"I'll fix you right up."

When Kelly reached beneath the front seat, unearthing an industrial-size bottle of hand sanitizer, Hank bid a wistful goodbye to a pleasant fantasy that started with licking chocolate frosting from her fingers and led who knew where. *Steady there,* he told himself as she squirted gel into his palms. He and the slim blonde might have been lovers once upon a time, but that was long ago. For now, they'd settled on being friends.

Was that the kind that came with or without benefits?

For good or for bad, there was no time to find out. The first of the crew arrived, dismounted and gathered around. Hank shot Kelly a wide grin as she was all but trampled in the stampede to the back of the ATV.

"You'd think they hadn't eaten in days, but they polished off their bag lunches less than an hour ago. Honest," he whispered while the boys wiped out a big supply of cookies, brownies and donuts. A chorus of polite "Thank you, ma'ams" soon filled the air. As quickly as they had come, all but one re-mounted their horses and headed back to work. Hank's chest tightened. Keeping his distance from Kelly would be so much easier once she jumped in the ATV and headed back to the house. But it was only neighborly to see her off, wasn't it?

He swung into Star's saddle again. From a safe distance he stared down at the woman who stirred more inside him than he liked to admit.

"Want to ride with me?" He bit his lip, but it was too late. The words already floated in the air.

"Only one problem, cowboy." Kelly's teasing green eyes smiled at him. "I don't have a horse."

"Josh." Hank turned toward a ranch hand who lingered at the back of the ATV. "How'd you like to take Ms. Kelly's four-wheeler and scout the trail to the Barlowe place this afternoon?" According to the notes Colt had left, the kid was something of an ornithologist. "I hear Barlowe spotted some kind of rare sparrow down near the Glades. You might want to check that out on your way back."

"A Cape Sables?" Josh asked. A ray of pure sunshine broke across the young cowpoke's face. He hurried to his horse like a man who feared the boss might change his mind. "Let me get my glasses."

Binoculars in hand, he passed the reins to Kelly. "If you don't mind, ma'am, leave Storm here in the corral when you get to the house. I'll swap the four-wheeler for him on my way back."

Hank pulled his feet out of the stirrups, suddenly restless as the teen rode off. At Josh's age, he'd still been floundering around, uncertain about much of anything except that both his marriage and his rodeo career had hit the skids. He wondered if the kid realized how lucky he was to find a way to combine his passion for birds with a job he liked.

Will I ever get that lucky? he asked himself, while he waited for Kelly to join him.

When she did, he turned away from his problems and clucked to Star. With Kelly riding beside him, they headed for a portion of the pasture he hadn't yet scoured for cows. On the way, he tried out a couple of conversation starters. Rehashing the past seemed like a sure-fire way to ruin the day. As for why they couldn't try again, he already knew the answer to that one. She was chomping at the bit to get back to Houston.

"You get to ride much in Texas?"

Kelly squared herself on the saddle. "Believe it or not, I mostly travel from my apartment to my car, or from my car to an office, where I push far more paper than I shovel hay. I hadn't been on horseback in ages till I came ho—" she hesitated "—till I came back here.

I'd forgotten how much I love all this." She swept a hand through the air. "Being outside, tending to the livestock."

She didn't exactly sound like someone who was all fired up about returning to her job in the city. Hank raised an eyebrow. Was she having second thoughts about leaving? About going through with the sale that would earn him a big commission?

"For five seconds there, when I was pulling that calf from the water, I considered not going back to Tallahassee. Considered staying here." He felt the corners of his mouth head south. What had started out as a way to encourage Kelly to stick to the plan had turned into a conversation far more honest than he'd intended. Uncertain which one of them he was trying to convince, he continued. "It didn't take me long to realize it'd never work."

"Why not?" Kelly asked as they neared a dozen head that had separated from the main herd. Hank sent the dogs in to get the cattle moving. Tail swishing, Kelly's mount settled in beside him.

"Not enough money in it," he admitted, opening up in a way he'd never been able to with Ty. Or with his brothers for that matter. But then, Kelly had always had that effect on him.

"I guess that depends on how much you need, doesn't it?"

She was right, but he gave his head a slow shake. "I'm pulling down a reasonable salary as the manager of the Circle P. The job comes with food and lodging so I can save some. But I'm only filling in for Randy and Royce till the New Year. Once they take over, it's back to real estate for this cowboy." He plastered a wide smile over his uncertain future. "I have Noelle to think about."

"You could buy your own place," Kelly suggested. "Make a permanent home for her."

His laugh rose and quickly died. Land, enough land to ranch, cost a whole lot more than the spare change he had jingling in his pockets. Or the meager savings he had in the bank. Not that he'd ever admit how far he'd fallen. But once he used his portion of the Bar X sale to get back on his feet, maybe he could save for a spread of his own. It was something to consider, though there was no rush. For now, a beautiful woman rode at his side, soft breezes cooled his face, tack jangled and leather shifted, providing background music.

He and Kelly soon settled into a once familiar rhythm of riding and talking. Kelly hadn't forgotten a thing about roping and riding in her years away from the ranch. By mid-afternoon they had cleared their section of wandering cattle.

"Let's call it a day," Hank suggested. "This was No-elle's first day at school. I want to meet her bus," he explained in answer to Kelly's quizzical look.

"You're making some headway with her."

At the compliment, he sat taller in the saddle. "I'm trying."

He was trying to avoid Kelly, too, but helping her down from her horse seemed like the gentlemanly thing to do. And once she was in his arms he had to kiss her....

LEAVING THE gelding to his dinner, Kelly toted the mare's feed bucket to the next stall. "Time to eat, Lady. You ready?" A slender equine head appeared over the Dutch door. Kelly lowered the pail to the floor and tugged a sugar beet from her pocket. She broke it into pieces, her eyes crinkling as soft lips politely lifted a chunk from her open palm. The good-natured horse nudged her shoulder.

"Sorry we missed our ride today," she murmured as she handed over another bit.

The mare needed a good workout, one Kelly'd had every intention of giving her. But, thanks to Hank, her plans had changed. And while she couldn't ignore the guilty twinge that stung her midsection whenever she considered her neglected chores, she didn't regret a minute of the afternoon she'd spent with the handsome cowboy. Or the kiss that had followed.

She rubbed her lips, which still tingled even though he'd left hours before. *Get a grip,* she told herself. The man could kiss the socks off a nun, but *her* delicious shivers probably had more to do with the Mexican takeout she'd brought home from Okeechobee and reheated in the microwave.

She swept a look through the barn she and Hank had spent the better part of a week putting to rights. In his stall, the gelding nosed his feed bucket. Grain shifted. The mare lipped another piece of beet from her open palm, impressive molars sounding a muffled chomp. And for a while, Kelly simply stood there, soaking in the sounds of home.

She'd miss this when she left, she admitted. The gelding's stubborn streak was far easier to handle than her usual impossible deadlines. Her feet felt better in a pair of worn work boots than the ones with fancy stitching she wore on sales calls. Even after all the years away, she gripped a curry comb with more confidence than she did a cell phone or laptop.

At length, she scratched the horse's silky forelock.

She frowned at the thought of leaving her grandfather's horses behind when she headed back to Houston. Or worse, splitting up the pair. The gelding and the little mare should grow old in a pasture together.

Could she take them with her? She brushed her hair over her shoulder, discarding the notion as quickly as it had occurred. Once she reported back to work, she'd plunge into a schedule so jam-packed she'd barely have time to eat and sleep, much less take care of animals that needed regular workouts and daily grooming.

Outside, a door slammed. Kelly eyed the feed bucket she'd left on the cedar planks near the stall. "Give me a second to see who's come to visit, will ya, gal?" She gave the mare the final piece of sugar beet and dusted her hands on her jeans on her way to the door.

Hank? This time she couldn't deny the thrill that raced through her. She ran a hand over her braid, which he'd loosened while treating her to a world-class kiss. He strode closer, making her wish she'd taken the time to shower and change clothes after a long afternoon of rounding up cattle.

She gave herself a shake. Considering she still had stalls to muck and horses to tend to, that idea rated high on the ridiculous scale. Hank was her neighbor and her business partner. She lifted a hand to her lips, but caught herself and instead gave her braid a tug. Okay, make that a neighbor with kissing privileges, but nothing more.

"Hank?" she asked, deliberately steering her thoughts to other reasons that might have brought him to the Bar X before sunset.

He lifted his hands in a sign of surrender. "Noelle's in such a foul mood I thought I'd better get her away from the Circle P before she wore out her welcome…

permanently." His downright sheepish look did funny things to her heart. "I didn't know where else to go."

Kelly waivered, torn between reading Hank the riot act for assuming he could dump his problems on her and helping the girl whose saucy attitude reminded her of herself at that age. "She have a rough day at school?" she asked, her chest tightening.

"Beats me." Hank shrugged his massive shoulders. "She's givin' me the silent treatment."

Kelly pushed past, her focus honing in on the child in the front seat of his truck.

"School?" she asked softly. She propped her folded arms on the window frame. Before her mom had left her in her grandfather's care, she'd lost count of the times she'd had to walk into a classroom where everyone else knew each other. Being the odd girl out was never fun.

"I hate it there." Noelle's chin wobbled in earnest. "The classes are dumb. No one talked to me. Or sat with me at lunch."

"Jimmy didn't eat with you?" Ty's son had promised to look out for her.

"He's second period. I'm first." Noelle's lips twitched. She plucked at her jeans. "He saved a seat on the bus for me."

"Well…" Kelly searched for reassuring words and came up empty. She pictured the girl alone at one of the endless cafeteria tables while all around her kids swapped milk for juice, chips for cookies and regaled one another with stories about their weekends.

"I'm never going back to that stupid school again."

Hank edged closer, bringing with him memories of how he'd come to her defense when she was the new girl in town. "The first day is always the worst," Kelly insisted. "It *will* get better."

Noelle mulled the idea over, her arms crossed. At last, she tipped up a tear-stained face. "You're sure?"

Rather than answer the child directly, Kelly asked, "You didn't see *anyone* you might like?"

Noelle picked at a spot on her jeans. "Riley Mattox lent me a pencil in Ms. Ellison's class."

"That'd be Lester's youngest," Hank offered from over her shoulder. "You remember him. Couple of years older than us? He hung around with Garrett."

"Well, there you go." Kelly leaned away from the window. The Mattox family owned a ranch on the other side of town. They were good people. "What do you want to bet that at supper tonight Riley told her folks all about the new girl in her class? I can practically see them talking about the good times her daddy had with your uncle Garrett growing up."

"And tomorrow Riley will ask you to sit with her at lunch," Hank chimed in.

"You think?" Noelle brushed the tears from her eyes.

"That's what your daddy did for me," Kelly answered.

"He did?" Noelle's gaze swung to Hank and back. "I guess I could give it one more day." She reached for the door handle but hesitated. "All the kids were talking about some stupid rodeo next month. What's up with that?"

"The Junior Rodeo in Keenensville," Hank put in.

"Yeah." Noelle nodded miserable. "*Everybody's* riding in it."

Kelly folded her arms across her chest. She tapped one boot against the hard-packed dirt while she gave

Noelle's lean build a once-over. She snapped her fingers. "You ever think of barrel racing?"

"Like you showed us the other day?" Interest glinted in Noelle's eyes.

Kelly nodded. Hank had created a make-shift course while she spoke with Ty on Sunday. When they were finished, she'd raced the gelding around the cans until the horse tired. "Want to try it?"

Brightening, Noelle looked past Kelly's shoulder to her dad. "Can I?" she asked.

Kelly held her breath. Teaching his daughter how to barrel race would require Hank's time and effort as well as her own. Was the rancher who'd had so little to do with his only child up to the challenge?

The air grew still while he studied the sparkles in Noelle's eyes. Whether he was unwilling or unable to break the connection, he spoke without lifting his head. "The barrels you used when you were training, are they still in the shed out back?" When Kelly reckoned they were, he continued. "I'll set 'em up while you two saddle the gelding."

"Lady would be a better choice. She hasn't eaten yet." For Noelle's benefit, Kelly explained, "I fed the gelding a little while ago. It's not good to exercise a horse too close to a meal."

The girl caught on right away. "It's like staying out of the water after you eat."

"That's right."

Kelly added a helmet to the gear they grabbed from the tack room. "I don't know this mare real well," she explained. "I'm not sure she's ever raced before."

But Lady settled that question as soon as they led her into the ring. Where the big gelding had done everything Kelly asked of him, the little mare practically chomped at her bit the minute she spotted the barrels in the corral.

"Somebody's done this before," Hank commented. Eager to go, Lady pricked her ears forward.

As surprised as he was, Kelly nodded. She'd have to check the records, but she'd bet money her grandfather didn't even know Lady had trained for the rodeo when he bought the horse at the livestock auction. With a good grip on the chin strap, she walked horse and rider through the course. After the third trek around the barrels, she released her hold. "Okay, now you do it."

As Noelle took her place behind the imaginary starting line, Kelly climbed to the top rail of the corral where Hank waited. She gave his thigh a reassuring pat when he claimed he was too nervous to watch, but grinned when she caught him peeking. When he scooted close enough that she felt him hold his breath, she stayed put to lend support to the anxious father. She hid a smile at the way Hank flexed his fingers when, after watching Noelle walk around the barrels a couple of times, she gave his daughter the go-ahead to pick up the pace. When Hank slipped his arm around her waist, she denied the small thrill it sent through her, telling herself he was only reaching out for something steady and familiar.

On their first try, the horse and rider trotted through the cloverleaf without knocking down a barrel. Kelly turned to Hank.

"She got the hang of it quickly, didn't she?" All the girl and horse needed was a little bit of practice and they'd be ready for the rodeo.

"She's a natural. Like you," Hank whispered.

For a second, she caught the flicker of something not at all connected with his daughter in his eyes. She practically shivered, but the moment passed as Noelle lined up for another run. Kelly forced her focus to the horse and rider in the corral. Offering pointers from her own days in the rodeo, she had Noelle and Lady chase the cans until they were both winded.

"Okay, that's enough for tonight," she called, just as the sun kissed the horizon. "Lady needs her dinner and a good brushing before bedtime."

"I'll do it." Noelle volunteered without being asked. "Me and Lady have some plans to make." She gave the horse a pat. "We're gonna be in the rodeo. And we're gonna win."

Kelly chortled. Hank's daughter had no shortage of confidence, she'd give her that. One practice session, and the girl was already dreaming of gold belt buckles. Not that it should have come as any surprise. After all, she was her father's child, and Hank had always known what he wanted.

She eyed Hank. Oh, he wanted her, no doubt about it. And she wanted him, too. But what was the point? They had no future together. In less than a week, she'd be back in Houston, while…

"So, I can ride her in the rodeo next month, can't I?"

Kelly stared at Noelle's glowing face. Her stomach dropped. What had she been thinking, getting the girl's hopes up? A month from now, Lady would be munching grass on someone else's ranch. Some other child might be putting the horse through her paces, but it wouldn't be under Kelly's watchful eye because she'd be gone.

Hank must have noticed the stricken look on her face, because the rancher stepped in front of her, buying her time to regain her composure. "We'll see about the rodeo, Noelle. Let me make sure there's still time to register. If we miss out on this one, there'll be others. Lots of them."

Turning to Kelly, his expression grew solemn. "Looks like my daughter is in need of a horse. Preferably one trained for barrel racing. You wouldn't happen to know of anyone who has a horse like that for sale, would you?"

"You'd buy Lady for her?" Kelly's heart stuttered. As a child, she'd known better than to even hope for such a gift. Instead, she'd competed on horses borrowed from the Circle P. "But she's only going to be here for a couple of months."

Like lightning on an open plain, a frown flickered across Hank's face. When it cleared, he shrugged his pair of impressive shoulders. "There's only one Lady, and there are a lot of summer vacations between now and the day Noelle goes off to college. I plan to spend every one of them with her. I'm going to save up to buy a place of my own, but till I do, we'll spend summers and school breaks on the Circle P. Meantime, if my piggy bank takes a hit, so be it. Seeing that smile on her face is worth more than all the money in the world."

Kelly stared into Hank's clear blue eyes. Was it possible he loved his daughter enough to sacrifice his own dreams for her? Her childhood sweetheart was turning out to be quite different from the man she'd always thought he was. True, he'd let her down once upon a time. And his parenting skills still needed some work. But just when she thought she had him nailed down, he did something she didn't expect. Something that forced her to see past the years he'd spent away from Noelle

and gave her a glimpse of the caring father he was trying to be.

Careful, she warned herself. *You don't want to make
the mistake of falling for him again.*

But would it really be a mistake?

And in that minute, she knew. Knew that while she'd
been focused on her grandfather and Hank's daughter,
the man she'd sworn she'd never love again had stolen
her heart.

Chapter Eight

Hank straightened, rolled his shoulders and resettled his hat. Man, what he wouldn't give for a long, hot soak. He massaged the achy spot in the center of his back while he swept a look over the unwavering flatness of the Bar X. Despite a gray sky, heat shimmered, creating distant mirages in the open fields. His gaze landed on the woman who leaned down from her saddle to open the gate into the ranch's southernmost pasture, and his gut tightened.

How could Kelly look so damned cute? Didn't she realize what misery she was putting him through?

After five long days rounding up cattle, Kelly's muscles had to be crying out the same way his were, didn't they? Maybe more, considering the years that had passed since she'd done any serious riding. Though she hadn't voiced a single complaint, he wondered how she'd react if he invited her to join him in the hot tub on the Circle P after they gathered the last of the strays that afternoon.

"What's the head count now?"

Hank blinked away the daydream. Heat pressed down on him. Humidity and dust stirred by several thousand hooves thickened the air. Grit coated his hands and face. Still, the image of him and Kelly separated by nothing but bubbles and water lingered. He blinked again, trying in vain to loosen his tight hold on the all-too-pleasant picture. Behind him, she hauled the gate closed.

He should have asked about the hot tub earlier. Regret whispered through him for not coming up with the idea before their time together had grown short. Once they began the long trek to the Barlowe ranch in the morning, it'd be days before he'd have another chance. By then, she'd be packing up and leaving again. This time, to head back to her life in the big city.

"The count?" she prodded. Cow dogs zigzagged back and forth beside the dozen cattle they had rounded up on another foray into their assigned section.

"That makes nine hundred and eighty-four head. How many did you say Paul had on the books?" Hank waved his hat, encouraging the new additions to join the main herd.

"A thousand and six." Kelly tossed her braid over her shoulder. "But if he kept records the way he kept track of everything else on the ranch, I wouldn't put much stock in that number."

Hank sucked on the inside of his cheek. Twenty-plus cows were too many to leave unaccounted. Along with his crew, he and Kelly had scoured every inch of the Bar X's four thousand acres. They'd searched behind every tree, ridden through dense patches of palmetto, followed every stream and circled every pond. He tugged on the reins, aiming Star for the gate. "I'll be horsewhipped if I can figure out where the rest of those strays are hiding, but let's give the area around the slough another look."

"Now?" Kelly asked as their horses plodded through the marginal grass while the dogs ranged ahead of them. "You don't want to call it quits for the day? Noelle's bus will be along soon, and I need to visit Pops later. Besides, I think we're in for a blow."

Hank glanced at the glowering sky. The thick cloud cover made it difficult to judge the sun's height. "Relax," he said, with more confidence than he felt. "We have plenty of time." He pushed his hat off his face and blotted his forehead with a bandana. "Have I told you how much Noelle and I appreciate the riding lessons?" Since Kelly had begun teaching his daughter the basics of barrel racing, there'd been a noticeable improvement in the girl's attitude.

"Only about a billion times," Kelly quipped. Her expression turned pensive. "You're sure the weather will hold another couple of hours?" The slough was nearly an hour's ride to the east.

"I checked the forecast before we headed out. This cloud cover should burn off, leaving us with bright sunshine straight through the weekend."

"I'm pretty sure the weatherman's aim was off this morning."

The joke was an old one—something about how the newscasters determined their predictions by throwing darts at a board—and his lips tightened into a thin line. With the Atlantic on one side and the Gulf of Mexico on the other, rain was the only certainty in Florida's otherwise fickle weather. The low clouds scuttling across the sky proved his point. He let his gaze drop to the herd they'd gathered in the section closest to the Barlowe ranch. Though one or two nosed the ground around the last silage tube, most of the cattle lay on the ground. The cows lowed, one loud *mrruh* blending into the general chorus.

Okay, it probably was going to rain, but a little water never hurt anyone.

To show he could be a good sport, Hank reached into his saddle bag and pulled out a poncho. He kneed Star closer to Kelly. "You can put this on if you want." He held out the slicker.

Kelly lifted an eyebrow, giving him a look he recognized from their childhood. Lady sidestepped out of reach. "I'm not afraid of getting wet if you aren't," she said, just as the first drops splattered her cowboy hat. One of the dogs whined.

The poncho draped across his saddle, Hank urged Star into a trot. "Let's make tracks, then. We'll check one last place and be home before you know it."

But they only made it halfway across the field before the wind picked up. The air grew so close and so thick Hank could practically feel the barometer dropping. Regretting the decision not to head for the barn, he shook his head.

"I'm thinking we're in for a gully washer," he shouted over a gusting breeze. "Aim for the trees." A quarter mile away, a thick stand of Australian pines offered more protection from the elements than they'd have on the wide-open pasture. He urged Star into a ground-eating lope while the dogs raced on ahead.

Despite the faster pace, they were still a hundred yards from the tree line when the rain began pelting down in heavy, wet sheets. The grass flattened beneath the deluge. In seconds, water plastered his shirt against his chest, soaked his jeans. It poured off the brim of his hat, creating a miniature waterfall that ran down his back. As if that wasn't enough, the temperature fell as the superheated ground soaked up the cooler moisture.

Ahead, the dogs darted under low-hanging branches. They shook themselves and, with their noses to the ground, set off to explore. Slowing Star to a walk, Hank guided the horse into a break between the trees. Within seconds, Kelly did the same. He led them deeper into the makeshift shelter to a spot where the rain barely dripped from overhead limbs. Star and Lady stomped and blew air, their tails swishing. Guilt tugged at his midsection when he realized Kelly's thin blouse had gotten drenched. A steady trickle ran from her water-logged jeans to the tips of her boots before splashing onto the carpet of pine needles. Her pale features peeked out from beneath her Stetson, making her look like a forlorn waif.

"Hey, now." He couldn't have that. He swung down from Star. "Give me your reins." When Kelly handed them over, he tied the little mare to a sturdy tree branch. "Here, let me help."

He'd only meant to lend a hand. Obviously, though, he hadn't considered the consequences of filling his arms with the living, breathing woman of his dreams. The brush of her body against his sent a current straight through him. Soaking wet, her shirt molded to her like a second skin. Her teeth chattered. The chill bumps on her arms sent his stomach into a spiral.

"Jeez, Kel." He held her at arm's length. "You're a block of ice. We've got to get you warmed up or you'll be the first person in Florida to ever die of hypothermia."

"I'm-m-m o-k-k-kay," she managed.

His stomach twisted in earnest. This vulnerability

was so unexpected, he didn't know quite how to handle it, so he did the only thing that came to mind. He wrapped his arms around her and drew her close.

"I'm sorry, Kelly. Sorry for everything." The long line of mistakes he'd made with her stretched clear back to the day she'd given him the wonderful, awful news that she was pregnant.

Beneath the pines, very little rain filtered through a dense roof made of boughs and palmetto fronds. The drops that made it through landed on the thick bed of pine needles with a soft tapping sound. He didn't know how long they stood there, holding each other, while his mind played the "What If?" game, taunting him with questions for which there were no good answers.

What if lightning had accompanied the rain and the rising wind? What if Kelly had been caught out in it because he was too stubborn to give up on a few cows that probably didn't exist anyway? What if, all those years ago, he'd hung on to her?

Pressed to his chest, she sniffled. He tightened his grip on her and drew in a deep breath. "This was all my fault. I should have listened to you. Should have headed in when you first suggested it."

Kelly tipped slightly reddened cheeks to his face. "Well, I did sort of dare you a little."

Was that forgiveness he saw dancing in her eyes?

The temperature had dropped steadily, but it wasn't the cold that spread goose bumps across his shoulders and down his arms. He owed that to new possibilities. He nuzzled her neck, a delicious warmth stirring low in his belly. Kelly smelled of soap and lilac. The scent mingled pleasantly with the crisp, clean smell of pine.

"Kelly?" he whispered.

Her face flushed with a glow that told him she felt the same way he did, but her jaw firmed. Her lips pursed. "We'd better get back to the others."

Hank's hands dropped from her waist. He knew that look. He'd seen it before. She'd worn it when she had overruled his objections and insisted on a surprise party for his sixteenth birthday. She'd sported it again the night she'd broken things off with him.

The woman had a stubborn streak, he'd give her that. But they weren't teenagers anymore. He was older now and, he hoped, wiser. They could be more than friends. They could have a future together. He tried to stare into her green eyes, but they wouldn't meet his own. "What is it? What's wrong?"

He might as well have poured a bucket of ice water over her head for all the good his questions did. Kelly's face shuttered. "We can't," she whispered, backing out of his arms. "We can't do this."

"Kelly, I know I don't deserve it, but I feel like we've been given a second chance, you and me. If you don't want it, if you don't feel the same way I do, just say it now and we'll forget this ever happened."

"It's not that. It's just…" Her voice trailed off while her features twisted, as if she were teetering on the edge of tears. "I can't afford to get involved with you again, Hank. We both have lives elsewhere. Neither of us is going to stick around."

It didn't have to be that way. She'd stepped out of his arms, but she hadn't turned him down, not completely. He grabbed hold of that thought and held on to it. He wanted her. More than anyone he'd ever wanted before. More importantly—at least to his heart—he'd fallen for her. He prayed she felt the same way.

The rain had stopped. A breeze rattled the limbs overhead, showering Hank and Kelly with droplets. Thin beams of bright sunshine filtered through the pines and palmettos. It was time to move on...wherever they were headed. They'd made a mess of things once before. If they didn't get it right this time, they'd never have another chance. But, unlike the last time when he'd foolishly walked away from her, this time, he wasn't going anywhere.

LADY TOSSED HER HEAD. Her ears flat, the sturdy little mare danced sideways. Kelly loosened her tight grip on the reins. She drew in a steadying breath, hoping to tame a fine tremble which had nothing to do with the sudden drop in temperature and everything to do with the handsome rancher riding beside her. The one she'd fallen in love with all over again, despite her best efforts to keep her distance.

When he'd held her beneath the trees, it had taken every lick of strength in her considerable arsenal not to kiss him. But she knew from experience that kissing Hank would never be enough. She'd never felt so safe, so loved, so accepted as she had when she was sheltered in Hank's arms. She wanted more, wanted him to complete her as no other man had ever done. But he'd fooled her once before, tricked her into believing they'd have forever together. And though, lately, everything she learned about him practically shouted that he'd changed, she had to be sure before she gave into her feelings.

As much as she wanted to, she couldn't forget the night she'd gone to him—two parts scared, one part thrilled—with the discovery that she was pregnant. And

he had let her down. That night, she'd hungered for reassurance. For Hank's arms around her. For promises
that they'd always be together, no matter what. But the
unmistakable *anger* that had flooded Hank's face had
shaken her love for him. And the accusations, the questions that had followed had only confirmed her worst
fears. He hadn't been in their relationship for the long
haul. He had wanted his freedom more than he'd wanted
her, or their baby.

She had tried her best to fall out of love with him
ever since. And had failed. No matter how much she
wished it, she'd never loved another man the way she
did him. Now that they'd been given a second chance,
could she trust him to stay by her side?

Throughout the years she'd spent on the Bar X, Pops
had regaled her with stories of how the men on the Circle P had chosen the easiest path. They had put themselves first, without caring for the needs of others, he'd
insisted. As an example, he'd cited the time a Tompkins
had wanted to draw more water from the Kissimmee
River. Their downstream neighbors had objected stren-
uously, concerned more about their own water rights
than anyone else's.

Hank's reaction to the pregnancy, combined with
his utter relief when she told him she'd miscarried, had
supported her grandfather's claims. It had shown her a
side of Hank she hadn't wanted to accept.

Yet, despite the hard feelings between their families,
Hank had saved her grandfather's life. He'd worked double time, making repairs on the Bar X while holding
down his day job at the Circle P. Thanks to the effort
he'd put into it, what had started out as a rocky relation-

ship with his daughter was developing into something more than either of them had thought possible.

But was he in it for good? Or would he send his daughter packing the moment his ex returned from her cruise? And what about her own relationship with Hank? If they gave it another shot, would he turn his back on her whenever life got hard?

She glanced twenty yards to her left where Hank scoured the brush for strays. She brushed tears from her eyes before they could leave telltale tracks down her cheeks. The man she loved had changed, and she wanted to give him—to give them—another chance. If she was wrong, if she'd misjudged him, he'd break her heart all over again. But wasn't it worth the risk?

Lowering her hand, she caught the slightest bit of movement at the edge of a palmetto thicket. Fronds rustled as she urged Lady through the waist-high brush.

"Hank, you gotta see this," she called.

Looking as if they were simply soaking up the rays instead of hiding out from the ranch hands who'd spent the better part of five days searching for them, a dozen head of gray Brahman stared at her from the other side of the thick brush.

"Well, I'll be," Hank said softly as he pulled in beside her.

"What do we do with them now?" Kelly asked. It'd take hours to move the cows into the pasture where they'd gathered the rest of the herd.

"We can't leave 'em here." Left to their own devices, these stragglers would probably disappear into the brush again. Hank loosened his rope from his saddle.

Kelly shielded her eyes from the sun, which had re-appeared from behind the clouds. So bright it was practically white, the fiery globe sank toward the horizon. "With the cattle drive starting tomorrow, I need to see Pops sometime today." Though he probably didn't know or care that she'd come, she had been doing her best to visit her grandfather daily.

"How 'bout this. You meet Noelle's bus and take her with you. I'll finish up here." Hank signaled the dogs, who rushed to work as if they had to make up for not finding the missing cattle on their own. The cows sang an unhappy chorus as, one by one, they lumbered to their feet.

"Promise her a candy bar," Hank shouted over the din. "She won't put up much of an argument." He whistled and twirled his lariat, herding the cattle at a steady clip toward the far pasture.

It might take more than a candy bar to make up for missing our barrel-racing practice, Kelly thought. Their daily lessons had progressed so well that Noelle had a good chance of bringing home a blue ribbon from the upcoming rodeo.

Too bad I won't be here to see it.

Her heart stuttered when she thought of all the things she'd miss by returning to Houston. Hank, of course. Noelle's first appearance at the rodeo. Her grandfather's continued recovery. She'd miss the land, too. Rising early and taking her coffee out to the front porch. Mucking stalls, and smelling sweet, fresh hay. Seeing the tiny shiver of pleasure that ran down Lady's neck when she worked a curry comb through her long mane.

Stockpiling memories she could pull out and reexamine during occasional breaks in her hectic schedule, she reined Lady toward the ranch house. There, she took a quick shower, managing to climb into her truck just as a big yellow bus turned off the main road. Dust rose in its wake. Clenching her teeth on a bone-rattling ride, Kelly reached the end of the drive with seconds to spare. She flagged down the driver.

Shouts, laughter and the happy banter of kids ready for the weekend flowed through the windows as Noelle skipped down the steps. The girl tossed her backpack into the wheel well of Kelly's truck and slid in, still waving to classmates who, only five days earlier, had given her the cold shoulder.

"Good day?" Kelly asked, though one look at Noelle's happy face made the question unnecessary.

Noelle snapped her seat belt. "Riley invited me to a sleepover in two weeks." She glanced into the backseat. "Where's Dad? He usually meets my bus."

"We found a group of strays that had been playing hide-and-seek with us." Kelly put the truck in gear. "He asked me to pick you up."

"Whew, what a relief." Noelle gave her forehead an exaggerated swipe. "I love him an' all, but he's not much help when it comes to clothes and stuff. What do you think I should wear to Riley's? Dad'll let me go, won't he?"

"I'm sure he'll say yes." In just a couple of weeks, both Hank and Noelle had changed considerably. He'd put some serious effort into becoming a better father, while his grumpy, challenging preteen had morphed into a fun, happy child. A child any woman would be proud to call her daughter. Kelly's throat tightened. As much as she loved Noelle, she couldn't become the girl's surrogate mom. Especially not since she'd be a thousand miles away by the night of the sleepover.

Noelle's eyebrows rose when Kelly turned toward the main road. "Wait. We're not going home?"

"I thought you could come with me to visit Pops." Kelly halted the truck at the stop sign. A right turn would take them toward Okeechobee. A left, to the Circle P. "I cleared it with your dad, but I can drop you off if you'd rather."

"Nah." Noelle settled into her seat. "That's cool." The girl launched into a recitation of the day's events, which lasted all the way to Okeechobee. Kelly soaked in every minute of it, knowing these moments would be something else she'd unwrap and relive during the long, lonely nights in Houston. At the rehab center, she sent Noelle off in search of the snack machine while she checked on her grandfather's progress.

"He's in the day room." An attendant with an armful of linens pointed toward the bright, airy room where a dulcimer band entertained the residents on Tuesday nights.

Kelly blinked. The gathering spot was beautifully appointed, but so far, her grandfather hadn't been aware enough of his surroundings to care. "When Noelle shows up, could you tell her where I went?"

"Sure thing." The attendant plopped clean sheets on the side table. She grabbed the remote and lowered the volume on the TV.

Kelly's boot heels sent tiny bursts of sound bouncing off the walls of corridors wide enough to accommodate wheelchairs and walkers. A hollow spot opened in her heart as she trailed her fingers along the handrail the doctors said her grandfather would never be well enough to use. At the door to the day room, she paused, her hand on the doorjamb. His broken leg propped on an extension, her grandfather snoozed in his wheelchair while around him other patients played board games or worked jigsaw puzzles on sturdy tables. Surprised that he'd improved enough to sit upright, she looked closer. Sure enough, thick bands belted him in place.

She crossed the room and pulled a chair up beside him. "Pops?" she whispered. "How are you doing today?"

Unlike other times when he'd slept through her entire visit, Paul snorted. He managed to raise his head, though it listed to one side. He looked at her, and in that second, Kelly prayed for recognition, for some sign that he knew who she was. A soft sigh escaped her lips when he stared past her. Disappointment coated the back of her throat, and her voice stretched thin. They'd never had the chance to heal the breach between them. From the look of things, they never would. Kelly gulped. Working to summon up enthusiasm, she brought him up to date on all that was going on at the ranch.

She wasn't sure how much of her talk he absorbed, but she kept at it. She was nearly finished when Noelle bounded into the room with all the exuberance of youth. Her fast pace, in a room where people normally moved slower than snails, caught the attention of every eye—including Pops's.

Though his right side remained immobile, a crooked smile stretched across his thin lips. His good eye brightened. He thumped the arm of his wheelchair with his left hand.

"Cay-ee," he croaked. "Cay-ee."

Kelly stared in disbelief as she glanced from Noelle to her grandfather. It couldn't be. She brushed the thought away as Noelle slid into an empty chair on her grandfather's good side.

"Hi, Pops," she said. "Look who's awake."

"Cay-ee, ay yoo faa cwa?" Paul stared expectantly at the young girl.

"Whatever, Pops." Noelle shrugged without any sign of malice. "I brought you a popsicle." She shot a look at Kelly. "I asked the nurse. She said it was okay."

Plastic crackled. More gently than Kelly could have imagined, Noelle held the cold treat to Paul's lips. His mouth dropped open like a baby bird's. Red liquid dribbling from one side of his mouth, the old man chortled and chewed.

Kelly grabbed a handful of wipes from a nearby dispenser. While Noelle jabbered on about school and new friends, they took turns feeding and blotting. By the time they finished, streaks smeared his shirt, but Pops was more alert than he'd been since the stroke.

They'd barely finished when the attendant came to wheel him to his room for dinner.

"Looks like you've already had dessert," she joked, unlocking the wheels. "That's a very pretty granddaughter you have, Mr. Tompkins."

Kelly started to correct the caretaker, but stopped when the world shifted under her feet. She shook her head, trying to make sense of her grandfather's reaction to Noelle.

"Gotta go now, Pops. Don't you give the nurses a hard time while we're gone." Noelle bent to kiss Paul's sparse white hair.

Later, Kelly wasn't quite sure how her grandfather managed to reach out his good hand. Work-hardened fingers wrapped around Noelle's wrist. A hoarse whisper rose from his chest. "Iy luh yoo, Cay-ee. Luh yoo."

The girl blinked and held her ground, but Kelly nearly lost it as her own mind connected all the dots. Noelle's resemblance to her at that age was nothing short of uncanny, so it was small wonder Paul had mistaken the child for her younger self.

But he loved her? After all these years, he'd finally said it out loud?

Reluctant to leave, she trailed slowly behind her grandfather's wheelchair as the attendant moved him back to his room. Kelly waited until the staff settled their patient in his bed. She lingered, hoping he'd say something more. Instead, the squeak of rubber-soled shoes on the tiled floor outside the room was the only sound she heard, until a nurse at the door cleared her throat. Kelly turned toward her.

"Ms. Tompkins, do you have a minute?" She spared a pointed look at Noelle. "Alone?"

She had been so focused on her grandfather that it took a second for the woman's request to sink in. When it did, Kelly dug in her purse for change. "Why don't you get something from the machines, honey," she suggested, handing the money to Noelle. At the last minute, she added, "Anything but candy."

"They have chips."

The nurse waited until Noelle was halfway down the long corridor before she spoke again. "Ms. Tompkins, we're very concerned about your grandfather."

"Really?" she asked, surprised. "He seems so much better." Hadn't he just said the words she'd waited half a lifetime to hear? Apparently, the effort had tired him out, because Paul had fallen asleep, his head tipped forward, his chin on his chest. Kelly fingered a lock of her loose hair. "I'd swear he recognized us today. That's a first."

"We see this sort of thing from time to time. A patient will make what seems to be remarkable improvement. Too often, it's short-lived. Worse, it's sometimes a precursor to another event."

Kelly stilled. "You mean another stroke?"

The nurse's bare lips thinned. "In his weakened condition, the results might be catastrophic."

How could things get any worse? Her grandfather already needed round-the-clock care. Kelly sucked her lower lip between her teeth as she weighed the costs of another visit to the hospital and even more intensive therapy. Would selling the ranch be enough?

She drew in a deep breath. The only way she could swing more expensive care would be to get back to Houston as soon as possible. She'd worked hard to climb the ladder of success at Palmetto Boots and, even though she didn't always appreciate the long hours and impossible schedules, she had to take care of the man who'd finally admitted his love for her. She had to.

Chapter Nine

Flames crackled and smoke rose from the campfire. While marshmallows roasted on long sticks and the golden sun sank into purple clouds, Hank picked a few bluegrass tunes on his dad's old banjo. The sky was inky black and dotted with a million tiny stars by the time Josh warned everyone to look sharp as they covered the final leg to the Barlowe ranch. At first, Hank thought the boy had happened on a nest of rattlers during his survey. He swallowed a laugh when it turned out the kid was gaga over the endangered birds he'd found and didn't want anyone to disturb their nests.

But once the last gooey s'more had disappeared, Emma and her kitchen staff loaded up the chuck wagon. Ty carried a sleeping Jimmy to his truck, and the convoy pulled out. One by one, the ranch hands said their good nights and turned in.

Beside him, Noelle leaned her head on his shoulder. Hank slipped an arm around his daughter and drank in the moment. One minute, Noelle had been going on about Riley Mattox's upcoming sleepover. The next, she'd given up the fight to keep her eyes open. She squirmed closer, and he smiled. He turned to the slender blonde sitting nearby, her fingers wedged between her knees.

"Looks like she finally conked out," Kelly murmured.

"Best get her tucked in," he said, rising. After a full day on horseback, Noelle had surprised them all by staying awake as long as she had. But there'd be another long ride tomorrow and, at the end of it, a barbeque and dance. The child needed a good night's sleep or she'd be too grumpy to enjoy the fun. Hank scooped the featherweight girl into his arms before he pinned Kelly with a questioning glance.

"You gonna stick around a while longer?" He wasn't sure how he managed to sound so normal considering how much he had been looking forward to spending some alone time with her.

"I'll be here. We can talk."

Talking was good. Kissing was better. Maybe they'd do some of both, he thought, as several long strides took him to the tent the girls would share for the night. He settled Noelle on her cot and zipped the sleeping bag closed around her while he tried to figure out what Kelly considered so important they couldn't spend the time lost in each other's arms. Lately, he'd caught her staring off into the distance as if she had a big decision to make. Had she changed her mind about selling the Bar X? He shoved the ridiculous idea aside. She'd never undercut him like that, not after all the work he'd put in to fixing up the place. Especially not with a potential buyer flying down to see the ranch next week. But what did she want to talk about? Their past? Their future?

Uncertainty rumbled through his chest as he lowered himself onto the log beside her.

"You get Noelle all settled in?" Kelly asked.

"She didn't even blink. Just rolled over. She was snoring away before I even closed the tent flap." Luckily, the cold front had knocked off the worst of the mosquitoes. Otherwise, heavy canvas or no, they'd all have been pretty miserable.

"Girls don't snore." Kelly poked his ribs.

"I'm sorry to inform you, but this one does." He caught her offending finger and brought it to his lips. "She has since the day we brought her home from the hospital."

When Kelly's eyes darkened, he tried telling himself his touch had caused the change. Problem was, the simple explanation didn't fit. He rolled his shoulders while she took the lead.

"You and Amy were still together?" she asked. "I wasn't sure how long the two of you stuck it out."

The past.

Hank stretched his legs toward the fire. "Things were rocky. I tried chalking it up to the pregnancy. I hoped once the baby came, everything would smooth out. I was wrong." He planted his hands behind him on the log. Leaning back, he let his arms take the weight of his upper body. "Our problems only got worse from the moment we brought Noelle home. I stood it as long as I could." He hesitated. He'd never told anyone—not his dad, certainly not his brothers—the whole sordid story. "Noelle was three months old when I found out Amy had taken up with an old boyfriend."

Kelly sucked in a breath.

Hank held out a hand. "It wasn't entirely her fault. In a way, I'd been cheating on her all along."

When confusion drew Kelly's eyebrows together, he

rushed to explain. "Amy knew I never loved her. Not the way I loved you. The way I still do."

In his dreams, this was where Kelly moved into his arms and they sealed their commitment to one another. But life did its usual excellent job of throwing cold water on his fantasies. Instead of smothering him with kisses and I-love-you-too's, she tugged her braid between her fingers the way she always had when worry overwhelmed her.

"But you left Noelle."

He took a breath. "That wasn't my decision. Amy threw me out when I demanded a paternity test. Noelle is mine," he added firmly.

"Of course she is." Kelly stared at him. She gave her hair another tug. "But you left your daughter behind? How could you do that?"

"I'm not proud of it, but yeah." He rubbed his chest, where the pain of the choices he'd made still lingered. "Amy's family comes from old money. They have battalions of lawyers on retainer. It was clear real quick that I wasn't going to get custody. No matter what. Besides, a baby needs her mother." Even in his own ears, his excuses sounded lame.

He sucked down enough air to finish the story. "Amy took Noelle and moved in with her parents. To save money, I sold our house myself. Turned out, real estate was something I was good at. Before you could say *'Brahman bull,'* I'd earned my license, opened up one office, then another. The hours were long and hard, but with the money I earned I could afford to send Noelle to private school, give her the best of everything." His shoulders slumped. "It took my dad's death before I realized money was a poor substitute for seeing my daughter take her first steps, hearing her say her first words."

The band at the end of Kelly's braid snapped. She worked her fingers through the thick blond plaits. "All this time I thought you'd abandoned your daughter because you didn't want her." She seemed to shrink. Her voice dropped so low the crackling flames nearly devoured it. "The way you didn't want our baby."

"No, Kel," he protested. "That's not true."

"But you blamed me. You said I'd ruined your life."

Nausea rolled through him. He'd gone over that day a thousand times, wishing he could go back and change the past. But the news had hit him hard, and he'd reacted like a stupid teenager who'd just seen all his plans for the future stampede over a cliff. An hour later, he'd realized his mistake, but by then, he'd broken her heart, betrayed her trust in him.

"I didn't mean it, Kelly. You were my life. You could never ruin it."

Light from the fire reflected off the angry tears gathering in Kelly's eyes. She glared at him. "You were glad when I found out I wasn't pregnant. Don't try to deny it."

The air left him so quickly it whistled through his teeth. His throat thickened. "Yeah. Okay. For eight seconds, it felt like the weight of the world had been taken off my shoulders. A wife, a baby—I wasn't ready. At seventeen, who would be? But I know now that we would have made it work, Kel," he said, insistent. "We loved each other."

"I loved you. I wasn't sure you loved me. The minute I told you I was late, you started pulling away from me."

The urge to make this right between them, once and

for all, filled him. Once the initial shock had worn off, he'd known what he'd needed to do—get a job and support his family. He clasped her cold fingers and felt them tremble. "I see now how it must have looked, but I was working, Kel. Scrounging for every nickel I could get my hands on. If there were stalls to muck, I mucked 'em. If there were fences to repair, I fixed 'em. I picked up every odd job I could find, did everything I could to make enough money to take care of you, of us. I talked to Dad about working full-time on the Circle P after high school."

Misery painted her cheeks with more tears, but she met his gaze. "You never said a word."

"I didn't think I needed to. We loved each other. We were gonna have a baby." Only things hadn't turned out the way he'd thought they would. He shrugged. "We never talked about what happened. How you…lost it."

Kelly's voice steadied. "My grandfather found out that I was pregnant. He flew into a rage. He'd always had a temper, but I'd never seen him so angry. He said all kinds of vile, hurtful things. About me. About you. That night, I miscarried."

Not a breath of air rustled through the palm fronds. The flames in the fire pit died down. The stillness stretched out, unbroken. Hank tried to breathe. His lungs refused to cooperate. As much as he wanted to draw Kelly to him, his arms hung from his shoulders like lead weights. His heart slowed until each beat reverberated through his chest.

"Why didn't you tell me? I'd have—"

"—blamed me the way he did?" Kelly swallowed. She stared down at her lap. More tears pooled in her eyes until they seeped from the corners and ran down her cheeks. "I was so messed up," she whispered between quiet sobs. "Pregnant. Scared to death. Then the baby was gone and my grandfather was ranting and raving about how I'd let him down. I didn't know what to do, where to turn. So, I did the only thing I could. I told you I never wanted to see you again. I thought maybe Pops would get over being mad at me, but he never did. Then, you went off rodeoing and married Amy. And Pops kicked me out anyway."

Hank struggled to his feet. At first, his legs shook like a newborn calf's and he wasn't sure he could move. Somehow, he made it as far as the other side of the clearing. He stared into the inky blackness beyond the campfire, his fists clenched. He wished there was someone or something he could punch. His thoughts collided. She was wrong. He'd never have left her. He turned to tell her as much.

Kelly sat, her shoulders hunched, right where he'd left her.

He hurried to her side and swept her into his arms. "I'm sorry. So sorry," he groaned. "I wish I'd been a better person. I wish you could've trusted me. We couldn't have changed the outcome, but at least we'd have had each other."

"Can you forgive me?"

He stared into her doubt-filled eyes. She wasn't the one who needed forgiveness. He did, and he had one chance, only one, to convince her. On ranches across the country, boys dreamed of making it to Las Vegas for the National Rodeo Championship. His brother Colt had been good enough to go all the way. Hank had planned to follow in the older Judd's bootsteps.

"You remember when I won the Junior Division?"

He'd competed all year for the grand prize, a hand-crafted saddle. "I wanted to buy you an engagement ring, but as hard as I worked, I didn't have enough money. I sold the saddle the day after you told me you might be pregnant. I planned to ask you to marry me the night of the senior prom, but…" His voice whispered into nothingness.

"By then I'd lost the baby and we'd broken up."

Firelight reflected off Kelly's shimmering tears. He wanted nothing more than to brush them away, along with all her regrets. And all of his. He leaned down, grazing her forehead with a kiss.

"I love you," he whispered. His finger under her chin, he tilted her face to his. "Always have. Always will."

When she trembled, he leaned closer, ever closer, until his lips met hers. He traced his thumb along her cheek, stroking the soft skin of the only woman who'd ever truly owned his heart.

"I'm sorry, Kelly," he murmured. "I gave up too easily once. I won't ever make the same mistake again. Can you forgive me?"

"Only if you forgive me," she whispered in return.

He moved his lips over hers. He was certain he was the least deserving man in the world. Despite that, she opened to him. Tentatively, the tip of her tongue met his, but one soft caress was all it took to make her sigh into the kiss. His lips fused to hers. He possessed her mouth completely while heat pooled below his waist. When she buried her fingers in his hair, he wanted her more than he'd ever dreamed possible.

Her hands cupped his head, drawing him lower with an insistence he couldn't deny. His fingers shook as he slipped her top buttons free. Pushing aside the rough fabric of her shirt, he trailed kisses across the top of her lacy bra. She moaned his name, igniting flames he wasn't sure he could control.

With a dull thud, a log collapsed in the fire. Sparks shot into the air before slowly drifting back to earth. From a distance, he heard the voices of cowhands keeping watch over the herd.

Hank groaned. He and Kelly weren't randy teenagers. There'd be no slipping off to his tent and making love on a cot. He wanted their next first time, when it happened, to be special. Though it took every ounce of control he had and then some, he kissed his way back to her lips. An unsteady breath escaped as he broke away, while still holding her close.

"There's nothing I want more in this world right now than for you and me to slip off somewhere. I want to spend the whole night showing you how much I love you."

"But we can't."

Kelly's voice shook with the same disappointment he felt.

"We're not kids anymore," he said, running his fingers through her hair. "Rain check?" He pressed another kiss on her forehead. "Noelle's got that sleepover coming up. What say we go away together, just the two of us?"

His fervor took a hit when Kelly went completely still in his arms. "I won't be here," she murmured. "By then, I'll be in Houston."

The reminder dimmed the image he'd built of coming home to the front porch of a ranch house where Kelly and Noelle waited for him. His heart sank. Had he and Kelly missed their chance at happiness? He felt the flutter of her heartbeat beneath her ribs, heard her soft sighs. He wanted this forever. Whatever it took, he was willing to make it happen.

"Don't worry," he breathed into her hair. "We'll make it work. Long-distance relationships suck, but we'll find a way. If I have to, I'll move to Texas."

He blinked. As long as he was starting over anyway, why not do it in Houston? He might not have the same connections, and it might take longer to save for the ranch he'd dreamed of owning in Glades County, but Kelly was worth it. He wanted the next fifty years with her. Wanted the nights of long, slow love. Wanted Noelle's barrel racing trophies to line the walls of her bedroom down the hall from theirs. And, if they were lucky, they'd turn a spare room into a nursery. In their nineties, he'd hold Kelly's hand on that same front porch as they watched dust rise behind cars loaded with grandchildren or great-grandchildren coming to visit the ranch, coming home.

"We'll make it happen." He kissed the top of her head. "Whatever it takes."

STOPPING TO PULL a mouthful of grass here, investigate a palm frond there, heavy gray cattle plodded into Kelly's view. Outriders followed behind, their ropes and, in some cases, hats swinging. As the cattle passed, the dust began to settle, and Kelly lowered the bandanna she'd tied over her nose and mouth. Weight slipped from her shoulders like a heavy winter coat.

"Is that the last of 'em?" She looked for the Circle P ranch hand who'd drawn the short straw and brought up the rear of the cattle drive.

"Yes, ma'am." Javier swung his hat. "Get on, now,"

called the swarthy young man. He urged a curious calf away from a patch of wildflowers and onto Barlowe land.

Kelly glanced at the clicker she'd thumbed as every gray head crossed the fence line. "I counted one thousand five. Give that number to Mr. Hank."

At the pens, Tom Hastings, the new owner of the Barlowe ranch, stood opposite Hank, one counting cattle as they went in, the other as they emerged. If the numbers didn't match, hers would serve as the tiebreaker.

"You aren't comin', ma'am?" Javier reined his sturdy little quarter horse to a halt.

"I'll be along in a few minutes." Kelly blotted sweat and dirt from her forehead. "Thought I'd enjoy the view for a bit."

"It's just grass and scrub, ma'am." The boy spurred his horse toward the cows, which had moved on without him.

Just grass and scrub. And yet, the vast stretches of unbroken land held a special beauty. Just after dawn, she'd spotted a sleek panther on his way home from a night on the prowl. Even now, wildflowers added splashes of color to a grassy green palate. A rabbit streaked from one palmetto bush to another, while a hawk soared against puffy white clouds.

Her heart clenched. After she left this time, things would never be the same. She'd never sleep in her grandfather's house again. Never carry her coffee out to the porch to watch the deer parade past the salt lick in the mornings. Never wander into the barn to curry the horses after a long ride.

Once she had collected a check for the cattle, her job on the Bar X would be done. The therapists at the rehab center would work with her grandfather, helping him regain as much mobility as possible. The nursing home where he'd live out the remainder of his days already had a bed on hold for him. The next week, Hank's client would fly in to see the ranch. Once it sold, people would forget the long feud between the Parkers and the Tompkinses. If she returned, it would be as a guest on one of Ty's trail rides. Which wasn't the same thing as owning land that stretched out forever beneath the clear skies. Not the same thing at all.

Wiping her cheeks, she closed the gate behind her as she rode onto Barlowe property.

She hadn't gone very far when her cell phone's insistent pinging signaled a return to civilization. She scrambled for the holder at her waist. Her vision swam when a dozen missed calls from the same number appeared on the screen. She thumbed the button and braced for bad news.

"Y-yes," she managed.

"Ms. Tompkins, I'm so sorry." Her grandfather's nurse didn't bother easing into the truth. "Your grandfather passed during the night."

"What happened?" Kelly asked.

"Another stroke? His heart? No one can say for sure. He was sleeping peacefully when the staff did rounds at midnight. But when we checked on him this morning…"

"I understand." *Gone. In his sleep.* She registered the words. "What happens next?"

She cast a glance at the trail of hoof prints that led back to the Bar X. It'd take the better part of a day to cover the thirty miles to the house on horseback. Could she get a ride from someone on the Barlowe ranch? What should she do about the…

The nurse's voice brought order to chaos.

"There's no need to do anything right now. He didn't have much with him, but I'll box his things and keep them in the office until you can get them. We'll have one of the local mortuaries pick up the remains. Do you have a preference?"

She recalled the name of the funeral home they'd used for her grandmother. "Buxton's, I guess."

"We've worked with them before. They'll do right by Mr. Tompkins. I'll tell them you'll be stopping by in the morning to make the final arrangements."

"Yes. Thank you."

The details handled, the nurse murmured a final, sympathetic remark before she hung up. Kelly stroked Lady's mane while green grass and blue sky shimmered through her tears.

The cell phone pinged again. Certain the nurse had forgotten to deliver some important detail, Kelly swiped a finger across the screen.

"It's about time you answered. I've been trying to reach you for three days."

In sharp contrast to the nurse's soft voice, Randall Palmetto's abrupt tone filled her ear. Numb with loss, Kelly hunched over her horse. She'd grown accustomed to the quiet sounds of everyday life in the country, and tears streamed down her cheeks as she held the cell phone away from her ear. She scrolled through her missed calls without finding a single 713 area code. How had Randall tried to contact her? By carrier pigeon?

"What do you need?" she asked.

"It's the Ivey's account. They've moved up the timetable. They want their first delivery in thirty days. We need you here, Kelly. Pronto."

"I—I…" She bit back a sob. "I don't know when I can make it. My grandfather passed away last night."

"I'm sorry for your loss." The man, who had often claimed family came first at Palmetto Boots, did not miss a beat. "Look, getting back to work will be the best thing for you. Can you be in the office tomorrow?"

Kelly's mouth dropped open. Her jaw worked, but no words came out. She gathered the shreds of composure around her like a shawl and tried again. "I need a week to plan the memorial service and tidy his affairs."

If the long, empty pause wasn't enough of a clue, Randall's ominous throat-clearing certainly conveyed his displeasure.

"We can't wait that long. We need someone to step up to the plate today. Tomorrow at the latest. I'm sorry," he said, not sounding at all sincere. "I'm going to have to hand Ivey's over to someone else."

Her account. The one that would guarantee her place in the Palmetto *family.* The one she'd spent six intense months negotiating. The one that was supposed to provide the security she'd been searching for her whole life.

That account?

Her jaw tightened as she pulled herself upright. Stretched in front of her was all the security she'd ever need. The man she wanted to spend forever with was waiting for her on the Barlowe ranch. She loved Noelle like the daughter she'd never had. They could be her family, her real family. All she had to do was say the word.

Was she certain? She and Hank had spent the night talking, making plans for the future. A future her job in Houston would only complicate. She hadn't wanted to give it up then, but now, hearing the censure in Randall's voice, she knew she was making the right choice.

"I'm sorry you feel that way," she said calmly. She tapped a nail in the coffin of her career at Palmetto Boots. "You'll have my resignation on your desk by the end of the week."

Randall's bluster told her he hadn't expected her reaction, but Kelly refused to let his protests change her mind. She ended the call. When the same number appeared on her screen seconds later, she blocked it. She reined Lady for the Barlowe ranch, and the one shoulder she could lean on.

As she rode into the yard, an eager young cowboy ran forward. She dug a present for Noelle from her saddle bag and turned the horse over to the hand, who would load Lady into one of the horse trailers for the ride home. Swiping at her tears, Kelly went looking for Hank. She found him at the cattle chute.

He looked up from a clipboard, consternation marring the features she loved.

"Trouble?" she asked.

"Can't get the numbers to—" His voice died the moment he caught sight of her. "What's wrong?"

"My grandfather," Kelly managed as a fresh wave of grief broke over her. "He's gone."

"C'mere." The clipboard clattered to the ground. Without saying a word, Hank opened his arms wide.

She stepped into his comforting embrace. Her head automatically found the soft niche under his collarbone. She snaked her hands around his neck. He held her until the first wave of grief passed. When it had, she filled him in on the scant details.

Hank rocked back on his heels. "I'm so sorry, Kelly. We knew this day might come, but I'd hoped…" He rubbed his eyes.

She sniffed. There were worse ways to go than dying in one's sleep. Her grandfather could have survived for years trapped inside his damaged brain. But if he'd ever recovered enough to understand that he'd never again make it from the house to the barn without assistance, or see the world from horseback, well, she hated to think how he'd have reacted. She brushed away her tears.

From some distance away, one of the hands called, "Mr. Hank. Ms. Kelly. Mr. Hastings is waitin' on ya'll."

"Give us a second. We'll be right there." Hank's answer rose above her head. He leaned down. "You want to do this? I can take you home if you'd rather."

Kelly mopped her face. "I must look terrible."

Hank smoothed her hair. His fingers trailed across her cheeks. "You're always beautiful to me," he whispered. He blinked. "Does this mean you'll be sticking around for a few days longer?"

Kelly nodded. She took a deep breath. "Let's keep the news about Pops between us for now. No sense ruining the party for everyone else." As for her other news, the news about making a permanent home in Glades County, that could wait, too. At least until she figured out some way to turn the Bar X into a profitable ranch again.

She scanned her new neighbor's busy yard. Despite her tears, she took in the changes the owners had made to the place. Fresh white paint coated the rambling house. White-washed fences lined the graveled drive leading to the main road. The Brahmans had been let out onto a pasture so rich and green it contrasted nicely against the gray-sided cattle. Across the yard, barbecue-scented smoke rose from two portable grills. Long folding tables and dozens of chairs sat under a large tent. On the porch, a willowy woman in a denim skirt stepped to a mic as members of a country and Western band scurried about setting up equipment.

"Test. Test," she said.

An ear-piercing squeal erupted. From behind a bank of audio equipment, a man made a chopping motion. He adjusted a knob, and the woman tried again with the same results.

"Brad, you gotta fix that," she said, her voice light and melodic. She lifted a fiddle from a nearby stand and ran the bow over the strings. The opening notes of a familiar bluegrass song rang out.

Kelly blinked. "Hastings went all out for an end-of-the-cattle-drive party, didn't he?" The events were common, but this one seemed a bit over-the-top.

"I heard someone say he'd turned it into a ranch warming. I think he invited half of Glades County. There's enough meat on those grills to feed two armies."

She smoothed her shirt, resettled her hat. "Could you give these to Noelle while I pay my respects to our host?" Bright pink and sparkly, the new boots would be a big hit with Hank's daughter. "Meet up with you after?"

"I'll be here for you, always." With a chaste kiss, Hank promised he was a man who had forever on his mind.

Chapter Ten

Hank swirled his tea. Ice cubes clinked against the glass. Doing his best not to look the part of the concerned parent, he rocked the heels of his boots against a porch that gleamed with a fresh coat of paint. In the practice ring, where missing boards had been replaced, Noelle and Lady blazed out of the starting gate. At the top of the cloverleaf, horse and rider cut the corners so close it was a wonder neither slit a leg wide open on the barrels' rough edges.

"Hee-yah!" His daughter's voice broke the quiet of a Sunday afternoon at the Bar X. Noelle rounded the last barrel and streaked toward the finish line.

"Eighteen seconds!" At the gate, Kelly held up a timer. "Your best yet!"

Hank let out the breath he'd been holding. Eighteen seconds would never earn a gold buckle in Las Vegas, but it was certainly good enough to win a blue ribbon at the Junior Rodeo next weekend. He lifted his glass to the rider and her coach.

"That's what I'm talkin' about," he said, using a phrase that had, thankfully, replaced the worn-out *whatever* in Noelle's vocabulary.

While his daughter lined up for the next run, he

shifted his focus to Kelly. How long was she going to stick around? Three weeks before, she'd insisted every minute she spent at the Bar X jeopardized a big promotion. Yet a week had passed since the funeral, and his favorite cowgirl hadn't said a word about returning to Houston.

Not that he minded. He ran a finger around the brim of his hat. He enjoyed spending his evenings on the Bar X. While Kelly gave Noelle a riding lesson, he tackled one item after another on their repair list. Later, while his daughter tended to Lady, he and Kelly put their time alone to good use. Kissing, mostly, but there'd been some talking, too.

Lately, though, he couldn't deny the feeling that their time, like the chore list, had grown short. *Just a little while longer.* He exhaled as Lady thundered across the finish line again. A smile he wanted to see every day for the rest of his life broke across Kelly's face.

"Another great run," she called. She slipped the stopwatch into her pocket. "That's it for tonight." She retrieved the Stetson Noelle had lost on her last ride.

"Just one more?"

Hank snorted. Noelle's pleading tone was the same one he'd often used back when he ate, slept and dreamed rodeo.

"Nope." Kelly remained stronger than he would have. She handed Noelle the hat. "There are horses to tend to and stalls to muck, and you have a big day at school tomorrow. Didn't I hear something about a math test?"

Hank managed to hide a grin when Noelle dismounted, grumbling. Her heart wasn't in the litany of complaints, and everyone within hearing range knew it. Warmth spread across his chest as Kelly gave his daughter a few last-minute instructions. The girl loved barrel racing, but he wasn't kidding himself. He had Kelly to thank for his daughter's softened attitude. He shoved his hat back on his head while he considered how things might have turned out if she hadn't been around.

The fact was, she had been. And if he had his way, they would never be apart again.

Across the yard, Noelle led Lady to the barn while the woman who'd captured his heart headed his way. He tracked the sway of her hips, the sweet rise and fall of her breasts. Desire, hot and strong, lanced through him, and he swallowed. They were taking things slow and had shied away from sleeping together. Watching her approach, though, he wasn't sure how much longer he could wait to hold her in his arms at night.

It was time, he thought, to take things to the next level. But this time around, he'd do it right. First, he'd put a ring on her finger. He'd make it clear that he meant to spend the rest of his life with Kelly…even if they hadn't quite figured out all the logistics.

"Hey, cowboy." Kelly took the stairs two at a time. "What'd you think of your daughter?"

"She's lookin' good," Hank answered, trying hard to shake his pensive mood. He let his smile widen. "Her coach is looking even better." He stood to greet her properly by pulling her close. The situation called for a kiss, and he bent willingly to the task. When one wasn't enough, he stole a second. Both tasted of mint.

Getting lost in Kelly's arms would be easy to do, but he had things on his mind. When they both came up for air a few minutes later, he settled for holding her close enough to feel the rapid beat of her heart against his chest.

"You know I love you, don't you?" Now that they'd been given a second chance, he repeated the words as often as he could.

Kelly tipped her face to his. Her soft "I love you, too" poured into all his empty spaces, filling them completely.

"The rodeo is coming up this Saturday." Resting his chin on the crown of her head, he drank in air scented with things he'd always associated with the slender blonde—flowers and horses and sunshine. He wanted to wake up to that smell every morning and go to bed with it every night.

"Yeah, cowboy. Why do you think we've been training so hard?"

He brushed a finger along her cheek, tracing the fine outline of her jaw. "Noelle's got that sleepover at Riley's after." Which would provide just the chance he needed to put his plans in motion.

"Tell me something I don't already know." Kelly nestled closer. "Rodeo and Riley. Riley and rodeo. It's all she talks about these days."

"Do you, um, do you have any plans afterward?" Now that the moment was upon him, an unexpected nervousness swept through him.

"Are you asking me out on a date?" Kelly's green eyes searched his.

"I could be." He brushed a strand of silky hair from her face. "Are you saying yes?" Ty had offered to take their horse and gear to the Circle P for the night. His son, Jimmy, had entered the goat-tying event.

"Hmm." Kelly frowned. "That still leaves the little matter of Noelle's trophy. She'll want to see it the minute she gets home from Riley's."

The conversation had deviated from the script he'd worked out in his head, but Hank caught the teasing glint in Kelly's eyes. She was stringing him along. Making him ask, thinking he'd chicken out. But he was determined not to. Once, she had been his past. Now, she was his future. He was ready for the house with the white picket fence. He'd even trade his truck for a minivan. All she had to do was say the word.

"You're sure she's gonna win, aren't you, Coach? I might not bet the ranch on that." Though, having seen his daughter race, he wouldn't bet against her.

When Kelly shoved her shoulder into his, he surrendered. "Heck, she'll probably sleep with the darn thing." He had, with his first trophy. He was pretty sure Kelly had done the same.

"I thought maybe we'd head up to Orlando. Spend the night at one of those fancy resorts. Just you and me. What do you say?"

Kelly nestled deeper into his arms. "I'd like that."

He'd intended to ask her about selling the ranch, but her happy sigh put an end to the conversation. They could talk any time—over the phone, across the yard— but kissing? That required proximity. Besides, he admitted as he leaned to press his lips against hers, he was much better at kissing than he was at talking.

For a while they indulged themselves. Eventually, though, a loud squeak made them pull apart.

"We should oil those hinges." Kelly tugged her rumpled shirt into place.

"Nah, that's my Noelle-warning system." Grinning, he feathered a final series of kisses across Kelly's crown. "It'll be the last thing I fix before John Jacobs gets here."

Hank frowned as the soft, willing figure in his arms stilled. He didn't get it. Kelly should be over the moon about the businessman's visit, especially since he'd surprised them both by making a verbal offer on the ranch, sight unseen.

"Second thoughts?" he whispered, praying he was wrong.

"About you? Not one. Why, are you in a hurry for me to leave, cowboy?"

The smile Kelly beamed up at him chased away the worrisome feeling that there was something she wasn't telling him. But her home, her career, was in Houston. And though he hated to see her go, he couldn't ask her to give up her life there, any more than she could demand he quit real estate.

"Not on your life," he murmured, before stealing a last mind-numbing kiss while he chalked her sudden quiet up to the new challenges they'd soon face.

He made it back to the Circle P before he realized he'd never gotten answers to his questions. He shrugged them aside. There'd be plenty of time for that later. For now, he had reservations for a weekend getaway to make.

KELLY LOADED THE last box of macaroni and cheese onto the conveyor belt.

"Stocking up?" The friendly cashier ran a carton of strawberries over the scanner.

"Thought it was about time I stopped living on takeout." Since her arrival at the Bar X three weeks earlier, she hadn't seen the point of filling the pantry of her temporary home. But now that she had decided to stay…

"Will that be cash or credit?"

Kelly slipped a plastic card from her wallet and handed it across. She was staying, wasn't she? The choice was up to her. She could probably still get her old job back. While it was true she'd burned the bridge to her big promotion, an abject apology would go a long way toward getting her back in Palmetto's good graces.

But was that really what she wanted?

She waited while the bagger settled bulging plastic bags in her grocery cart. She couldn't picture herself leaving. Not now. Not with Noelle's first rodeo competition a few days away. But later wouldn't be any better. There'd be other rodeos, other competitions. She wanted to help Noelle through her first crush, first kiss, first breakup. To take her shopping for her prom dress, and to eventually help plan her wedding.

No, she told herself, stuffing the card and receipt in her purse. Going back to Houston wasn't nearly as important as it had once seemed. Repairing the Bar X's broken-down fences with Hank, riding beside him as they rounded up strays, sitting beside him at the campfire—she'd fallen in love all over again. And not just with the rancher. Through him, she'd rediscovered a love for wide open spaces, for watching the sun rise over a flat horizon. Life would never be the same without the nuzzle of a horse softly lipping carrots from her open palm, the honest burn that came from mucking stalls or toting feed buckets.

One of the front wheels on her cart wobbled as she pushed it across the parking lot. It took money to keep a spread like the Bar X afloat, but in a matter of weeks, she'd taken a child who'd never raced barrels before and turned her into a master of the sport. Working with Noelle had given her a sense of purpose she'd never got-

ten from her job with Palmetto Boots. So, she'd put her
business experience to work on the problem and come
up with a solution that would let her keep the ranch and
do work she enjoyed. Within a month, she could open
a training camp for rodeo riders. She'd offer classes in
barrel racing and pole bending, and by the end of the
year she could board her students' horses, too. If things
went as well as she thought they would, she'd owe Hank
a huge debt of gratitude for helping her turn the ranch
into her home again.

Not that a mere *"thank you"* would do. No matter
how much they loved each other, business was business,
and she'd promised him the commission when she sold
the ranch. Now that she planned to hold on to the Bar
X, she couldn't renege on their deal. Luckily, the pro-
ceeds from the cattle sale would more than reimburse
him for his time and materials.

Reaching for her keys, she brushed her fingers over a
check with Hank's name on it. She'd thought about giving it to him in person, but was afraid he might refuse
to accept the money. Lifting her phone, she punched
the number for Information, certain the receptionist
in Hank's real estate office could provide her with his
business address. She'd put the check in the mail to him
before she headed home to the Bar X.

Suddenly, she couldn't wait another day to tell Hank
about her change of plans. A warm glow spread upward
from her midsection as she imagined the look on his
face when she realized she was staying put. Sure, they'd
still have the hurdles of a long-distance relationship
to jump over once he returned to Tallahassee, but that
wouldn't be for a while. Until then, she'd only be as far
away as the ranch next door. Drinking in a breath of

sun-kissed air, she decided to head for the Circle P as soon as she unloaded the last of her groceries.

"HANK." TY'S VOICE caught him in the hall. "Just the man I wanted to see." His boss and longtime friend clapped a hand on his shoulder. "You missed supper again tonight. Chris tried out a new recipe. I swear if that boy keeps cooking the way he does, my wife's gonna put me on a diet." Ty patted a flat belly.

"Sorry I missed it." To get to Kelly's on time, he'd grabbed a PB&J on his way out the door.

Ty beckoned him into the office. "I spotted Noelle running up the stairs a minute ago. Didn't I tell ya once you pried her loose from her cell phone and MP3 player, she'd enjoy herself here?"

"Yeah. She's a different girl. It's hard to believe she was so aggravating at first." Hank raked a hand through his hair. "In fact, we're getting along so well I've decided to talk to Amy about changing our custody agreement." Now that he'd had a taste of fatherhood, he couldn't imagine going months without seeing his daughter again.

Ty shot him a questioning look. "You think she'll let Noelle stay on?"

"Noelle's not a baby anymore. She's certainly old enough to know her own mind. And she doesn't seem to have any problem voicing her opinions." That drew a laugh from the man seated behind the desk, and Hank chuckled. "I'm pretty sure, given the chance, she'd choose to stay through the end of the school year." He grinned. "As long as I have Lady." He waited a beat. "And Kelly."

"Oh?" Ty's brows rose so high a body would need

climbing gear to get over them. "You've fallen for her again?"

"Hard," he admitted. Harder than he'd ever thought possible. He let the seconds tick by. He'd kept too much bottled up for too long. He needed to talk things out. His eldest brother, Garrett, was his usual sounding board. But Garrett had his own worries—a troubled pregnancy, a wife on bed rest.

"She broke your heart once, man. I'd hate to see you get hurt like that again. You sure you don't want to slow down, take things easy?"

"Too late. I'm already gone." Hank gave his friend a sheepish smile. Yes, he'd loved Kelly when they were young and reckless. When he couldn't think straight enough to separate making love from being in love. It hadn't worked out then, but things were different now. And not just because they'd decided to wait until they were sure before they took the next step.

Ty's brows lost their mountainous quality. He drummed his fingers against the desk. "Have you thought all this through? You're talking about getting custody of Noelle. But isn't Kelly headed back to Texas? What will you do then?"

"After I finish out my stint at the Circle P, I'll follow her there." Hank stretched his legs as he tried the idea on for size. It wasn't a perfect fit. Going back to real estate, even for a little while, had put a nasty taste in his mouth. But to earn enough to buy his own ranch, that's what he'd have to do. Florida, Texas—where he was wouldn't matter, so long as he and Kelly and Noelle were together.

Which brought him right back to where the conversation had started—with Noelle.

"I have to work things out with Amy before I can do anything else." He meant to ask if Ty thought Sarah could help him. As a former social worker, he figured she might have a suggestion or two about the best way to approach his ex-wife.

"I think you're forgetting something." Ty traded his fingers for a pencil and continued drumming. "You have a home and a business in Tallahassee. You can't walk away from all you've built there."

"Yeah, well, about that…" Hank's shoulders bent under a weight he'd carried for too long. "To tell you the honest truth, I kinda fell on hard times in North Florida." At Ty's puzzled look, he hurried to explain. "I didn't want to say anything, but when the bottom fell out of the real estate market two years ago, people stopped buying. I kept things going as long as I could, tried my best to keep my head above water. In the end, there was nothing I could do. I had to close up shop. What you saw in my car when I got here, that's all I have left." Hank brushed his hair off his face. His friend would understand. Not so long ago, Ty had faced his own problems in holding on to the Circle P.

Ty whistled, long and low. "Man, that's rough."

"Yeah, well." Hank cleared his throat. "I'll be back on top again soon." Now that the market was on the rebound, an infusion of cash was all he needed to get started again. His share of the Bar X would do all that and more.

He paused. To excel, a broker had to be available for his clients 24/7. Which meant working nights and weekends. The very hours he had hoped to spend with Kelly and Noelle. Was that what he wanted?

He swallowed a bitter taste. He had to make the best

hand he could out of the cards he'd been dealt. And it was only for a little while. Just until he saved up enough to buy a spread of his own. A ranch Kelly could come home to each night. A permanent home for Noelle. A place where he'd raise and train horses—barrel racers and cutters for the rodeo. He pushed back the uncomfortable feeling that his idea had some serious flaws, and concentrated on how to make it work.

But Ty's interest had drifted to something behind the chair where Hank was sitting. He turned slowly, expecting to see one of the ranch hands or Jimmy in the doorway. The sudden appearance of Kelly startled him.

"Kel, what're you—" The smile he wore whenever she was around faltered as she sliced a hand through the air. Hank blinked at the hurt look on her face.

"I thought I could do this," she whispered. "I can't. Not now." She darted out of sight.

Feeling like he was missing a key piece in a puzzle, Hank listened to Kelly's boots echo down the hall. He swung to Ty. "How long was she standing there?" he demanded.

"Not long," Ty sighed.

Hank hit the rewind button, replaying the last part of their discussion. "Damn," he said softly. His stomach sank. Without bothering to say goodbye, he hustled out the door after the only woman he'd ever loved.

KELLY STOMPED TOWARD the front door, her boot heels sounding in sharp counterpoint to the painful ache in her heart.

"I should never have come here," she muttered. "Should never have thought…"

She cringed at her own stupidity. She'd been on the

verge of making the second biggest mistake of her life. The first being that she'd given her heart to a man she couldn't trust...again. Stumbling onto Hank's conversation with Ty had only confirmed what she'd already discovered—that Hank had been lying to her all along. He wasn't a successful real estate mogul in Tallahassee. She'd come to Ty's office determined to ferret out the truth. But one look at Hank and she'd known she wasn't ready to hear any more of his lies.

Why had she given him her heart again? She'd thought he'd been falling in love with her. But his focus hadn't waivered from the big commission he'd earn by selling her ranch, the land that had been in her family for generations. When she thought they were building a future together, he'd been planning to restart his real estate business, one she hadn't even known was in trouble. The whole time she'd spent confessing her deepest secrets to him, he'd been hiding his own.

A sob worked its way up from somewhere deep inside. She covered her mouth to muffle it. From behind her, she heard a familiar voice.

"Kelly. Kel, wait up."

Run! Run!

Twelve years ago she'd run far, run hard. She'd made it as far as Houston but, no matter how far she went, she hadn't been able to escape her past. Instead, she'd carried the pain of her broken heart, of their lost child, with her. Much as she wanted to put a thousand miles behind her tonight, she knew running away wasn't the answer now any more than it had been then. Summoning a strength she didn't realize she had, she swung around to face Hank.

She spun without warning and so fast she nearly

collided with the big man. The hands she'd dreamed of holding for the rest of her life landed on her shoulders. She flinched away.

"Don't touch me," she hissed, knowing her resolve would crumble if he held her. "I tried calling your office this afternoon. They said you'd gone out of business six months ago." His old offices now housed a dog grooming parlor. His phone number had been reassigned to a thrift shop. "Why'd you let me think you ran some hotshot real estate agency in Tallahassee?"

"I'm sorry you had to find out that way." He didn't even try to deny it, but his fingers jerked back as if he had just grabbed a hot pan from the oven. "I didn't want you to know. I didn't want anyone to know."

"You should have told me. You said you loved me. We were planning a future together. Isn't that the kind of thing you tell someone you love?"

"I planned to, Kel. I just hadn't…yet."

She backed away, putting some much-needed space between them. "I thought you wanted to help me and my grandfather. You said you were being a good neighbor. But you were using me all along, weren't you?"

"That's not true," Hank began in a far-too-reasonable tone. "The day we picked Noelle up from the airport I told you I wanted to list the Bar X. I offered to make repairs, pay for them out of my own pocket. In exchange, you said you'd let me handle the sale of the ranch. I've kept my part of the bargain."

He didn't say it was time for her to keep her half, but she understood. He expected her to do her part. "Yeah, well, things have changed. I don't need to sell anymore."

Hadn't that been the whole reason for the phone call that had knocked the wind out of her? She'd wanted to mail a check to his office. She'd imagined Hank's face lighting up when she told him she wasn't leaving. Instead of dancing with joy, though, his blue eyes darkened.

"What about your big, important job in Houston? The one you were so fired up to get back to?"

Kelly felt the color drain from her face. She could have rushed back to Texas immediately after her grandfather's funeral. If she had, she was pretty sure she could have reclaimed her job at Palmetto Boots. Instead, she'd stayed put, sacrificed twelve years of hard work for a chance at a future with Hank. But what kind of future could they have if it was built on lies?

"I—I quit. The important thing is that I was on my way here tonight to tell you." She laughed bitterly. "I've been feeling so guilty about not telling you right away, but you've been lying to me from the very beginning."

Hank's face hardened and his gaze turned icy. "You never intended to go through with the sale, did you? You've been planning this all along."

"No." She eyed him carefully. Hank had stood to make a lot of money from the sale of the Bar X. Was that what their relationship was really all about? Had he ever wanted her, just her? Or had he been more interested in her ranch?

"This isn't about me. This is about you. You're the one who never once mentioned you ran your business in Tallahassee into the ground." She forced herself to take a breath even though her chest felt so tight she wasn't sure she could breathe. "Did you ever love me? Or were you just taking advantage of what we once were to each other in order to get what you wanted?"

She had to face facts—Hank didn't want her any

more than her mother or her grandfather had. She'd
been a fool to think she'd find acceptance in his arms.
"I should have known better than to trust you, to trust a
Judd," she whispered. "After all, your family has been
taking advantage of mine for decades."

Hank's gaze hardened. "Spoken like a true Tompkins," he growled. "Always looking to blame the other
guy for your own mistakes."

Regret flashed across his face, but it was too late.
He'd gone too far, and so had she. They'd both crossed
a line neither of them could ever uncross. She stood,
a deadly calm replacing the emotions that had been
swirling around her. She reached into her pocket and
drew out a slip of paper. "You might as well take it," she
said, holding out the check. "It's all you really wanted."

"Keep it," Hank spat. His mouth worked.

Kelly braced herself for another harsh retort. But before he could speak, the clatter of running feet sounded
from the hall. Seconds later, Ty stood in the doorway,
his face pale.

"Hank," he blurted, unaware that her world had just
shattered. "Phone call."

Hank's jaw clenched. The veins in his neck stood
out. "It better be life or death, man."

"It's Garrett," came Ty's hoarse whisper. "And it is."

Hank took a single step toward the office. For a moment, he stood, rocking back and forth as if he couldn't
decide which of two terrible choices deserved his attention.

The broken shards of her future rained down around
Kelly. With one hand she motioned him away from her.
With the other, she shoved the slip of paper back into

her pocket. "Go," she told him. "There's nothing more to say here."

Slowly, the man she'd loved and lost, twice, turned and walked away. Unable to stand the hurt anymore, she did what she should have done in the first place. She ran.

Chapter Eleven

Careful to slide his bare feet across the boards lest he step on one of his brothers, Hank padded through the living room. The entire Judd clan had raced to Garrett's side the minute the call went out. No one had slept much those first few nights, but now, following the funeral, they were sprawled wherever they could plunk down pillows and grab a couple hours' sleep. Across the room, one of the twins snorted and turned over. Seconds later, his double did the same. Hank eased the back door open.

Few lights glowed in the neighborhood of older homes crowded cheek-to-jowl next to the freeway. Even at this hour, heavy traffic sped beyond the sound barrier at the end of the street. A horn honked. He heard the squeal of brakes and, for an instant, he held his breath. When the thud of smashing cars didn't follow, he picked his way across the patio.

"Couldn't sleep?" Garrett's voice rose out of the dark of the moonless night.

"Nah." Hank lowered himself into an empty lawn chair, the metal frame scraping across the poured cement. "You?"

"The baby woke me. Mom's givin' him a bottle."

In the four days since they'd brought Baby Boy Judd

home from the hospital, Doris had handled all the mothering duties.

"You decide on a name yet?" He couldn't be Baby Boy Judd forever. Now that Arlene had been laid to rest, Garrett's son needed a name.

The plastic webbing on Garrett's chair creaked. Hank caught a whiff of whiskey in the pause that followed.

"We were gonna name 'im Seth Arlan for our dads, but…"

Hank stretched his legs. "Those are some pretty heavy monikers to stick on the littlest Judd." His throat closed shut. In the past year, there had been too many losses. He coughed. "Maybe we could just call him LJ."

He had meant it as a joke, but Garrett raised his flask. "To LJ," he toasted, knocking back a swig. "You want a hit?"

"Nah, I'm good." The thinking he had to do was best done with a clear head. "You gonna be okay?" Concern for his brother welled up so high it damn near squeezed tears out of his eyes.

"It wasn't supposed to be like this, you know?"

The pain in the elder Judd's voice took a sledgehammer to Hank's heart. "I know, bro." Used to getting advice from his big brother, he didn't know what else to say.

"Sarah and Emma packed up Ar—her clothes. They dropped 'em off at Goodwill," Garrett said. He seemed to be avoiding using his wife's name. Maybe it hurt less that way. "Emma's been cooking up a storm. There's gotta be six months' worth of meals in the freezer." After a long minute, he added, "Mom's gonna stay on. Help with the baby, with LJ. I have six weeks' paternity leave…"

In the distance, a dog barked. Garrett fell silent.

"Sounds like you've worked out a plan." At least, a plan for dealing with *things*. Emotionally, though, Garrett was a wreck, and probably would be for a long time. A gaunt ghost of himself, the older Judd sipped quietly but steadily from his flask. He'd yet to hold his infant son or even acknowledge the baby's presence with anything more than a devastated look whenever LJ cried.

"You got anyone s-special in your life?" Garrett's words slid into one another as if they were skating on ice.

"I thought I did." How long had his normally buttoned-up older brother been bending his elbow? Long enough to empty the flask? Hank shrugged even though Garrett couldn't see the motion. "Things didn't work out."

"Next time, work harder." A damp hand clutched Hank's forearm. "You only get one chance. Maybe two. Don't waste it."

"I'll do my best." Reassurance rolled off his tongue, but inside his head a voice chided him for blowing his last chance with Kelly. He placed his hands on his knees and pushed himself out of the deep chair. "Now, what say we get you into bed?" A few remaining gulps sloshed against the flask's metal sides as Hank took it from his brother's limp hand and stuck it in his back pocket. "Need some help, or can you make it on your own?"

"I kin do it."

Though Garrett teetered for a second or two, he shuffled across the patio and down the hall on his own steam. After he watched him go, Hank lifted the flask to his mouth and took a single pull. The cheap liquor burned all the way down. Small wonder it had hit his brother so hard. He stepped inside and stashed the flask in a liquor cabinet.

His grief-stricken brother might have had one or two more than he should, but he gave solid advice. Too bad this time it had come too late to be of any help. Resigned to a life much emptier than the one he'd planned, Hank headed for the sleeping bag he'd spread out on the floor in the guest room. The world could come to an end but, back home, the cattle needed to be fed, stalls mucked and fences tended. He and Noelle were set to leave at first light.

In the morning, as dark-haired men with red-rimmed eyes loaded suitcases and bedrolls into trucks, Hank went looking for his daughter. As expected, she was in the baby's room, leaning over the crib. Tears streaked her cheeks.

"Oh, Daddy, he's so little." Noelle clutched one of the baby's stuffed toys so tight its eyes bulged. "How's he going to grow up without a mother? Why did Aunt Arlene have to die?"

Hank leaned over the crib rail to trail a finger over the sleeping infant's downy black fuzz. "It is sad, honey. A lot of people love this little baby, though." He caught the next useless platitude before it spilled across his lips. Despite all the love in the world, LJ would grow up missing his mother. He cleared his throat.

"Sometimes things happen we can't control. But Arlene wouldn't want everyone to be sad all the time. More than anything, she wanted this little fella to come into the world." *So much that she sacrificed her own life for his.* "She'd want us to love him and help raise him, don't you think?"

Not that he was going to be around to do his part. Once he and Noelle moved to Houston to be with Kelly... *Kelly.*

He had lost her for good this time. He'd said things he didn't mean, words he wished he could take back even as they'd echoed off the walls in the great room. He longed to take her in his arms and tell her how sorry he was, but he knew he'd never get that chance. She'd never give it to him. She didn't trust him. She'd made that perfectly clear. Without trust, they couldn't have a future together.

He wrapped an arm around Noelle's shoulders. "You still going to Riley's sleepover tonight?"

They'd skipped the rodeo—there would be others—but the Mattox girl had postponed her party for a week just so his daughter wouldn't miss it.

Noelle scrubbed her cheeks. "I guess. We can't stay here?"

"I'm afraid not. It's time to go. We're meeting Ty and Sarah at their hotel in thirty minutes." Ty and Hank and their families had caravanned to Atlanta together. They'd follow one another back to the Circle P, where an unsettled future waited for him.

Hank stared down at the baby. He'd let everyone think he was grieving for Arlene, when in all actuality, he'd been grieving for all that he had lost. The woman he loved. The chance to restart his business. Even his relationship with Noelle. He couldn't very well ask the courts to grant full custody to a dad who didn't have a full-time job...unless he stayed on as the manager of the Circle P. He had examined the possibility from all angles without finding a downside.

Determined to resolve the issue before they left Atlanta, he sought the twins. He found them milling about on the patio of the house, which had proven too small to hold five tall Judds, their assorted womenfolk and one newborn.

"So, Royce, Randy, I was thinking," he said, once they'd moved past the preliminaries. "How set are you on managing the Circle P after the first of the year?" He held his breath and studied his youngest brothers.

Randy gave his twin a sideways glance. "We were actually hoping—"

"—to talk to you about that." Royce finished his brother's sentence, as he always did.

"Things are going good for us in Montana." Randy scuffed a boot against the rough concrete.

"Mr. Sizemore asked us to stay on another year." Royce stared at the roofline as if he could see all the way to the north country.

"He's converting the ranch over to solar power and—"

"—offered us a big bonus if we'd stay on till he finishes the job."

Hank blinked. He'd always had trouble following the conversational ball as it bounced between his brothers. This was no exception. "You don't want to come back to the Circle P?"

Randy's lips twisted into a half-grin. "Oh, we do. We do. Just not this year. Maybe next December? Think you can stick it out that long?"

"Well…" Hank pretended to mull it over while he peered closely at his brothers. His mom had always known when Randy had gotten into the cookie jar by the way he flicked his thumb against his forefinger. The twins were now too old to look embarrassed over a few stolen cookies, but they'd inherited the same dark good looks as the rest of their brothers. And hadn't the boys let it slip that Sizemore had a couple of pretty daughters? He swallowed a smile. He'd bet the pot more than cattle and ranching was keeping the twins in Montana.

Well, good for them.

In a year, Noelle would be more settled, more grounded in school, and he'd have a better chance of gaining permanent custody. Another year of free room and board meant he could sock away most of his salary toward the ranch he'd buy one day. Someplace close enough that his daughter's aunts and uncles could be part of her life. He stuck out his hand.

"You've got a deal. I'll stay on for another year so you can…" He let his voice trail off, hoping the boys would supply a few pertinent details.

"Finish that power grid," said Royce.

Which left just one final loose end in a life that wasn't turning out the way Hank had wanted it to. Pain knifed through his chest. He wondered how long his heart would continue to ache. Resolving to carry the hurt for as long as it took, he squared his shoulders. No matter what, he couldn't let another dozen years pass before he made things right with Kelly. He had wanted her as his wife, his lover, the mother of his child. Maybe he couldn't have what he wanted but, now that he was going to stick around, he couldn't let the wound between them fester, either. If for no other reason than good neighborly relations, he had to apologize.

He felt for the metal band he'd tucked into the fob pocket of his jeans the first day he'd seen Kelly at the hospital. He'd carried it with him wherever he went ever since. Though it had lost its standing as a token of eternal love, he thought she might like to have it. Maybe, he told himself, maybe, it'd help them forge a new relationship from the ashes of the one they'd burned.

Could he be just friends with Kelly? He shook his head, knowing he'd never be able to look at her without seeing all they had lost.

KELLY SLID THE new sign welcoming guests and students to the Bar X into the bed of her pick-up truck. She'd been right to offer classes in pole bending and barrel racing. Three young girls had already signed up, and she hadn't even advertised yet. Heading for home—her home—she rolled down the windows and surfed one hand through the air. All things considered, she could make a good life for herself at the Bar X. Not the life she thought she'd wanted in Houston, certainly not the life she'd planned with Hank and Noelle, but a good life just the same. She'd be fine…as long as she didn't run into a certain tall, handsome rancher before her broken heart had a chance to heal.

But at the thought of Hank, her mood dimmed. She hoped he'd move soon. To Tallahassee or wherever. The more time they spent apart from one another, the better chance she had of getting over him. Shaking her head, she pulled her hand back inside and rolled up the window. They hadn't seen each other in more than twelve years after their last breakup. What made her think she'd do any better this time around?

For the time being, she'd do her best to avoid him. Not that it would be easy. She'd definitely have to stay away from the school, since Hank had taken an active interest in his daughter's education. Running into him in the hallway was sure to undermine her fragile recovery. Trips to the feed store were out. She refused to fuel the local gossip mill by breaking down between the oats and the barley if a certain rancher happened to walk in. As for Eli's, it was a good thing she still had that mail order account. In fact, maybe she would do all her shopping online from the comfort and safety of the Bar X.

But Hank had left his imprint on her ranch, too, she realized as her truck rumbled down the drive he'd smoothed and graded. Her foot slipped off the gas pedal the instant she spotted his familiar truck parked next to the house. Her breath caught when she saw his frame rocking on her front porch swing. Fresh tears welled in her eyes.

She brushed them away. Hope—tiny, flickering hope—rose within her as she removed the keys to her truck. Had he come to give them another chance? Was he as sorry as she was? She squelched the idea. Reaching for her purse, she positioned it like a shield of armor across her chest, as she latched on to the one topic that wouldn't lead back to *them*.

"I was so sorry to hear about Arlene," she said, stepping from the vehicle. "How's Garrett?"

For a moment, Hank's handsome face crumpled. "Lost. Devastated. Coping the best he can."

Sympathy shivered through her and she blinked.

"He's still Garrett, though. Still the brother who hands out good advice."

"Oh, yeah?" Unable to stand still and face Hank, she grabbed a couple of bags of groceries from the back of the truck. She made it to the steps before he took her packages from her and toted them up the stairs.

"He told me not to waste another minute." Hank

waited while she unlocked the door. "It made me realize how much time I'd—we'd—wasted."

Wasted? She wouldn't call it that. Not exactly. Yes, they'd spent twelve years away from one another, but despite their recent problems, she'd loved Hank every minute of every day for as long as she could remember.

He settled the grocery bags on the kitchen counter. He turned to her, his blue eyes searching. "I know I'm the last person on earth you want to see right now. You have every right to be angry with me. But I couldn't leave things the way they were between us. We did that once before."

Her heart pounding, she paused, waiting to hear what he had to say.

"I didn't tell you about the problems I ran into in Tallahassee. I should have, but I let my pride get in the way. I didn't want you to think any less of me. I don't know if it'll help now or not, but I didn't tell anyone—not even my brothers."

She wasn't at all sure why that made a difference, but it did. "Okay," she murmured as her pulse steadied.

"All I know is, I couldn't move forward without telling you how sorry I am."

Tempers had flared in the great room the other night. Not just his, but hers, too. She'd hurled accusations she didn't mean, said things she'd regretted ever since. If for no other reason, they needed to clear the air between them if they were going to live next door to one another for any length of time.

She was sure neither of them wanted to let their break-up rekindle the animosity that had been handed down from one generation to the next. What if, instead of starting a feud by cutting off his neighbor's water supply, her great-great-grandfather had simply talked to the Parkers and the Judds about drawing more water from the river? Would Pops have blamed the Judds for her grandmother's car accident if tensions hadn't already been running high between the two families? Would things have turned out differently for her and Hank if her grandfather had approved of their relationship? She drew in a breath that shuddered through her lungs, fanning the edges of her broken heart.

"I said some terrible things, too. Things I didn't mean." She started to explain, but stopped herself with a quiet admonition to keep things simple. "I'm sorry," she finished.

"Me, too," he rasped. "I never should have said…I had no right…"

"Shh," she whispered. Truth shone in his blue eyes. She had no need to dredge up the past, to analyze every accusation. "It's behind us now. We'll move on from here."

"So, we're good—you and I?" Hank asked. "Friends?"

Kelly's lower lip shook. Afraid the tremor would expose her raw emotions, she clamped her teeth down on it. Though she and Hank had made their peace, it would be a long time before she could look at him without wanting to inhale his musky scent or thrill to his touch. Not long ago, she'd thought they'd have it all…together. She didn't know if she could settle for friendship. But with no other choice, she nodded.

"My groceries are melting," she said, latching on to the first excuse she could come up with. "If that's all, I'll see you out."

The distress in Hank's eyes told her he'd seen her ploy for what it was. "If you change your mind about selling your grandfather's ranch, I can put you in touch with someone here in Glades County, someone who'll do right by you."

"My ranch," she corrected, though a guilty twinge sped through her midsection. Her decision to hang on to the Bar X had hurt him. She got that, though she'd never intended to shortchange him. "I still have that check for you—to cover your expenses and reimburse you for the time you invested here. It's on the table by the door." Secured by a paperweight, the slip of paper had been there for a week.

"So, you really are staying?" At her nod, he started, "Well, that'll be—" warmth softened his features before his jaw hardened "—awkward."

Keeping the ranch was going to mean many things—hard work, long days. Awkwardness wasn't one of them. "Why would it matter?"

"I told Amy it wasn't good for our daughter to move again before the school year finished, and for once she agreed with me. So, we're staying on at the Circle P for another year at least. It's the best thing for Noelle, and for me. I'll use the time to save up for my own spread. Someplace close. I want to give Noelle the same sense of family and community I had growing up. Besides—" he shrugged "—the twins need another year in Montana."

Confusion washed over her. She felt it creep onto her face. "You're going to ranch in Glades County?" So much for any hope that time and distance would heal her broken heart. With her luck, he'd buy a place smack-dab next to hers. She looked down, unable to understand why that possibility spread a healing balm across her aching chest.

"Colt wants to raise bulls for the rodeo. Once I have

my own place, I thought I'd throw my hat in with his. Only, I'll focus on horses."

"Huh." Kelly worried her bottom lip. It would take years for him to save enough cash to buy his own place. Meanwhile a few acres, the barn and practice rings were all her riding school required. It seemed foolish to let the Bar X pastures go to waste when Hank could put them to good use. And she did owe him more than she could ever repay by simply writing a check. Yet she hesitated, uncertain the facade of friendship he'd insisted upon would hold up if they had to see each other every day.

Hank cleared his throat. "I brought you something. Besides my apologies, that is."

"Yeah?" Shelving her concerns about the ranch for the moment, Kelly lifted her chin. Hank looked down at her, tenderness showing in his steady gaze. At first, she didn't notice the ring in his open hand. Or the tiny diamond chip that graced the gold band. When she did, an awe-filled "Oh!" escaped her lips. She reached out before she could stop herself and ran a finger around the circle.

"What is this?" she whispered, though anyone in their right mind knew an engagement ring when they saw one. Trouble was, she couldn't be sure she was in her right mind.

"It's the one I bought ages ago. For you. I just…never had the chance to give it to you."

"You kept it all these years?"

He shuffled, his boots scuffing the floorboards. "I tried not to. Meant to pawn it or list it on eBay or something. I never quite got around to it."

His voice dropped so low she had to lean in to catch his final words.

"Any more than I ever got around to getting over you."

She stared at the ring he'd sold his prize saddle to buy. The yellow gold was a little worse for wear, but then so was her heart. Both had survived some tough times.

"Anyway, I wanted you to have it. As a symbol of our—" Hank's ragged breath stirred the air between them "—friendship."

The block of ice surrounding her heart melted. Her final reservations slid away. She closed the gap between them, moving close enough that she felt the rise and fall of his chest, saw the tiny crows' feet at the corners of his eyes deepen, heard the soft intake of his breath. "And if I wanted something more than friendship? What if I wanted to wear this ring for real?"

She watched him struggle to maintain his stoic composure. His strong Adam's apple moved up and down. His jaw clenched. The muscles along his chin tightened. Still, she continued to hold his gaze. His eyes filled as he lost the battle. His face softened. He blinked and tiny drops clung to his dark lashes.

"I'd be the happiest man in the world," he whispered hoarscly. "But are you sure?"

"I've never been more certain of anything in my life," she said, shaken by the fact that he'd held on to the ring…and their love…for all these years.

As for herself, she had never let go. She knew she never would. Not when she'd finally found the love and acceptance she'd been searching for her entire life. It had been right where she'd left it all along, in the arms of her Glades County cowboy.

* * * * *

COMING NEXT MONTH FROM

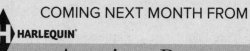

HARLEQUIN

American Romance®

Available November 4, 2014

#1521 THE SEAL'S HOLIDAY BABIES
Bridesmaids Creek
by Tina Leonard

Ty Spurlock plans to head out of Bridesmaids Creek, Texas, even though it means leaving his heart behind. Jade Harper knows he'll come back because she has a secret for him— and it's the best Christmas present of all!

#1522 THE TEXAN'S CHRISTMAS
Texas Rodeo Barons
by Tanya Michaels

Rodeo cowboy Daniel Baron has no desire for a family of his own. But when he falls for Nicole Bennett, who is pregnant with twins, he may have to change his mind!

#1523 COWBOY FOR HIRE
Forever, Texas
by Marie Ferrarella

When Connie Carmichael takes a job designing a hotel in Forever, Texas, she hires local Finn Murphy to help with the construction. But soon the cowboy carpenter is making designs of his own—on her heart.

#1524 THE COWBOY'S CHRISTMAS GIFT
Crooked Valley Ranch
by Donna Alward

Crooked Valley Ranch means everything to foreman Carrie Coulter, but to Duke Duggan, it's only a place to regroup after army life. They are at odds—until they rediscover their smoldering chemistry....

HARCNM1014

REQUEST YOUR FREE BOOKS!
2 FREE NOVELS PLUS 2 FREE GIFTS!

 HARLEQUIN®

LOVE, HOME & HAPPINESS

YES! Please send me 2 FREE Harlequin® American Romance® novels and my 2 FREE gifts (gifts are worth about $10). After receiving them, if I don't wish to receive any more books, I can return the shipping statement marked "cancel." If I don't cancel, I will receive 4 brand-new novels every month and be billed just $4.74 per book in the U.S. or $5.24 per book in Canada. That's a savings of at least 14% off the cover price! It's quite a bargain! Shipping and handling is just 50¢ per book in the U.S. and 75¢ per book in Canada.* I understand that accepting the 2 free books and gifts places me under no obligation to buy anything. I can always return a shipment and cancel at any time. Even if I never buy another book, the two free books and gifts are mine to keep forever.

154/354 HDN F4YN

Name	(PLEASE PRINT)
Address	Apt. #
City	State/Prov. Zip/Postal Code

Signature (if under 18, a parent or guardian must sign)

Mail to the Harlequin® Reader Service:
IN U.S.A.: P.O. Box 1867, Buffalo, NY 14240-1867
IN CANADA: P.O. Box 609, Fort Erie, Ontario L2A 5X3

Want to try two free books from another line?
Call 1-800-873-8635 or visit www.ReaderService.com.

* Terms and prices subject to change without notice. Prices do not include applicable taxes. Sales tax applicable in N.Y. Canadian residents will be charged applicable taxes. Offer not valid in Quebec. This offer is limited to one order per household. Not valid for current subscribers to Harlequin American Romance books. All orders subject to credit approval. Credit or debit balances in a customer's account(s) may be offset by any other outstanding balance owed by or to the customer. Please allow 4 to 6 weeks for delivery. Offer available while quantities last.

Your Privacy—The Harlequin® Reader Service is committed to protecting your privacy. Our Privacy Policy is available online at www.ReaderService.com or upon request from the Harlequin Reader Service.

We make a portion of our mailing list available to reputable third parties that offer products we believe may interest you. If you prefer that we not exchange your name with third parties, or if you wish to clarify or modify your communication preferences, please visit us at www.ReaderService.com/consumerchoice or write to us at Harlequin Reader Service Preference Service, P.O. Box 9062, Buffalo, NY 14269. Include your complete name and address.

HAR13R

SPECIAL EXCERPT FROM

HARLEQUIN®

American Romance®

Read on for a sneak peek of
THE SEAL'S HOLIDAY BABIES
by USA TODAY *bestselling author Tina Leonard!*

"Don't you have anything to say for yourself?" Jade demanded.

"I'm content to let you do all the talking." Ty settled himself comfortably, watching her face.

She sat next to him so she could look closely at him to press her case, he supposed, but the shock of her so close to him—almost in his space—was enough to brain-wipe what little sense he had in his head. She smelled good, like spring flowers breaking through a long, cold winter. He shook his head to clear the sudden madness diluting his gray matter. "You're beautiful," he said, the words popping out before he could put on the Dumbass Brake.

The Dumbass Brake had saved him many a time, but today, it seemed to have gotten stuck.

"What?" Jade said. Her mesmerizing green eyes stared at him, stunned.

He was half drowning, might as well go for full immersion. "You're beautiful," he repeated.

She looked at him for a long moment, then scoffed. "Ty Spurlock, don't you dare try to sweet-talk me. If there's one thing I know about you, it's that sugar flows out of your mouth like a river of honey when you're making a mess. The bigger the jam, the sweeter and deeper the talk." She got up, and Ty cursed the disappearance of the brake that had deserted him just when he'd needed it most.

He smelled that sweet perfume again, was riveted by the soft red sweater covering delicate breasts. "Okay, fine. Everything is fine."

"It's not fine yet." She smiled, leaned over and gave him a long, sweet, not-sisterly-at-all smooch on the lips. Shocked, he sat still as a concrete gargoyle, frozen and immobilized, too scared to move and scare her off.

She pulled away far too soon. "*Now* it's fine."

Indeed it was. He couldn't stop staring at the mouth that had worked such magic on him, stolen his breath, stolen his heart. He gazed into her eyes, completely lost in the script.

"What was that for?"

Jade got up, went to the door and opened it. Cold air rushed in, and a supersize sheet of snow fell from the overhang, but he couldn't take his eyes off her.

"Because I felt like it," Jade said, then left.

Look For
THE SEAL'S HOLIDAY BABIES
by TINA LEONARD
Part of the BRIDESMAIDS CREEK *miniseries*
from Harlequin® American Romance®.

Available November 2014
wherever books and ebooks are sold.

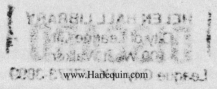

www.Harlequin.com

HARLEQUIN®

American Romance®

A Love Built To Last?

Finn Murphy has always been good at building things.
So when the town's alluring new developer makes him
an irresistible offer, he's all set to jump on board. And
working side by side with Constance Carmichael sure has
its perks. Too bad the big-city beauty will be heading back
East after she makes her name in his hometown.

Look for
Cowboy For Hire
by MARIE FERRARELLA

Part of the *Forever, Texas* miniseries from
Harlequin® American Romance®.

**Available November 2014 wherever
books and ebooks are sold.**